A MARGINAL MAN

Bernard Brachya Cohen

A MARGINAL MAN

Copyright © 2014 by Bernard Brachya Cohen
Edited by Jeremy Sandlin
Cover Copyright © 2014 by John Phillip Cameron
ISBN-13: 978-1623750770

Publisher's Note: This is a work of fiction. All characters, places, businesses, and incidents are from the author's imagination. Any resemblance to actual places, people, or events is purely coincidental. Any trademarks mentioned herein are not authorized by the trademark owners and do not in any way mean the work is sponsored by or associated with the trademark owners. Any trademarks used are specifically in a descriptive capacity.

First Edition
Visit our website: www.mquills.com

A MARGINAL MAN

For Amy, Emily and Selma.

COHEN

.

PART ONE
Chapter 1

The psychology faculty meetings took place in a classroom across the hall from the department office. Kramer and six other members of the department sat in chairs usually occupied by their students, with the chairman, Tom Bordman, seated in front of the blackboard in his shirtsleeves, his heavy body partially hidden behind the wooden instructor's desk.

This morning, Bordman was interrupted by a hesitant knock on the door. The department secretary, who had instructions not to interrupt faculty meetings unless the reason was an important one, knocked again, louder, then opened the door and tip-toed into the room. She bent over to whisper to Bordman, and together they glanced in the direction of Kramer. As their eyes caught his, Kramer felt a sudden twinge of anxiety; he was no longer a professor but a pupil at his desk, about to be summoned to an unknown fate.

"A call for you, Dan."

He took the call in the secretary's office. It was his wife.

"I'm sorry," she said. "I had to talk to you."

"What is it?"

"Lance."

"Can it wait? I'm in a faculty meeting -- can I call you back?"

"No." There was a quaver in her voice. "I'd like you to come home."

"Why?"

"I found some things in Lance's drawer," Claire said. "I'm sure he stole them."

"What things?"

"They're silver. They look valuable -- like antiques. Something you'd see in a museum. I wondered if I should call the police."

"No," Kramer said. "Claire -- don't do that. I'll handle it as soon as I get home."

"By then he'll be back from school. He might leave and we won't know what's going on until it's too late. We've got to talk to him as soon as he comes in."

"I'll see what I can do."

"Dan, I don't want to have to face this alone. Can you come home now?"

Kramer hesitated. As chairman of the department faculty selection committee, he was due to give a report on his interviews with candidates for a vacancy in the department. Leaving now would be awkward and difficult to explain. Kramer suspected that his wife was overreacting to something trivial, yet he knew her tolerance for Lance's behavior had grown very thin. She might call the police after all.

"I'll leave right away."

He hung up the phone but remained seated, his blank gaze fixed on the desk. He imagined Lance standing in a prison cell, gripping the bars and staring at him with a look of disbelief.

The office was suddenly warm and Kramer felt perspiration rising on his forehead. He removed his glasses and reached into his back pocket for his handkerchief; holding the glasses close to his eyes so that he could see them, he wiped the lenses until they were clear.

He went back to the meeting, interrupting Bordman's discussion of course offerings. "It seems there's a problem," Kramer said, standing in the doorway. "I have to go -- I'm sorry."

Bordman gave him a quick goodbye nod.

Chapter 2

He stopped at his office to drop off his lecture notes and books. Rather than take the elevator, Kramer headed for the stairs to save time. The hall was empty and silent; he could hear his colleagues lecturing behind closed doors.

The office had been his for almost twenty years, ever since his arrival at the college. Tiny and windowless, with a standard wooden desk, two chairs, green file cabinet, an overhead fluorescent glare, a cork bulletin board and a No Smoking sign in twenty languages, the office and its sparse furnishings had remained the same while he gradually changed; his black hair had thinned, his beard was now almost all gray.

He dropped his things on his desk. As he made his way to the stairs the silence in the hall was suddenly broken by scattered shouts and bursts of laughter. Classes were changing and Kramer was soon engulfed by a wave of students. One or two called out,

"Hi, Professor Kramer!" Preoccupied with his son, he forced himself to nod and smile.

Outside on his way to his car he passed groups of students, nodding to those he recognized. Gusts of wind blew swirls of leaves into the street; the tangy smell of fall was in the air. The drive was short -- he lived close to the campus. The image of his son came to him again, arousing familiar feelings of affection and concern.

Kramer drove along Main Street, past the town's bank with its white Ionic columned facade, then past the steepled Presbyterian church with its arched red door. He turned down Latimer Street to a part of town with rehabilitated brick row homes where many of the college faculty lived. Usually Kramer walked to the college; he took the car when he had an extra load of books, or when it rained or snowed.

 Pulling up in front of his house, he saw his wife standing behind the storm door waiting for him. As he came up the steps, leather brief case in hand, she pushed the door open.

"Am I glad to see you," she said. He dropped his brief case on the hall table and immediately followed her up the stairs to Lance's room; it was in disarray as always, with clothing piled on the chair and bureau, car magazines scattered on the desk, and sneakers and socks on the floor near the unmade bed. Claire opened a bureau drawer and removed several thick woolen sweaters.

"Look," she said.

He glanced at the drawer contents, saw a number of silver objects and felt a pang of recognition, as if discovering the photograph of a loved one long gone. Removing an ornamented rectangular piece with a silver chain attached at two corners, he said,

"These are Torah ornaments."

Claire nodded. "I thought it might be something Jewish. What is that?"

"The breastplate, it's attached to the Torah with this chain."

He felt his heart beating more rapidly, and as he rested the breastplate on Lance's bed he thought that this might be the worst thing his son had done. He reached into the drawer again, and with a tinkling sound lifted two long silver pieces decorated with filigree and tiny bells. Claire held them, listening to the musical sound.

"They're beautiful."

"Finials," Kramer said. "They go on the end of the two wooden rollers."

He carefully placed the finials on the bed alongside the breastplate. Claire asked,

"Is there anything else?"

Kramer found one remaining item, almost hidden along the edge of the drawer -- a slim, scepter-like object less than a foot long.

"Oh," Claire said. "There's a tiny gold hand at the end."

The hand had an extended index finger. "It's a Torah pointer, used by the reader as a guide."

Claire examined each of the items more closely.

"I'm sure he stole them."

"Let's not jump to conclusions. There may be some explanation. I hope there is. We'll just have to wait and see what Lance says."

He returned the ornaments to the drawer and Claire covered them with Lance's sweaters. They went down to the living room to wait for their son.

Chapter 3

As they sat in silence, Claire curled up in a corner of the sofa and Kramer in his recliner, he thought of the early years, the happy time with his son. Kramer remembered his open admiration of the boy's sturdy legs, assured gait and physical strength. Again and again he would say to his wife, "Just look at him!" Lance quickly took to sports as he grew older, excelling in baseball. Sitting in the bleachers in the town park, Kramer could watch his son for hours.

The confident boyness, the robust physicality – these traits were so unlike his own when he was a child. Whenever he saw his son's assurance and grace on the playing field, Kramer recalled his own experience as a poorly coordinated boy, blind without his thick glasses. He saw himself standing with his elementary school classmates in the chilly schoolyard during gym, watching the captains -- always the same two quietly confident boys -- select their teams.

The best athletes were picked first, then the captains moved down the line, choosing this boy then that, "I'll take Collins,"... "I'll take Freed,"... "Hartman,"... "Johnson".... Soon only the weakest players remained, the dregs. Feeling increasingly exposed as the number dwindled; Kramer yearned for the ordeal to come to its familiar conclusion -- his standing alone, picked last with grudging reluctance.

But that was not the end; drawing ever closer would be Kramer's turn at bat. As though obeying some unspoken directive, the boys on the opposing team all moved in from the outfield, almost on top of him, a semicircle of vultures waiting for him to strike out. Gripping the bat he wished that this time his myopic eyes and unresponsive arms would somehow coordinate, that the bat and ball would connect, shocking them all. But that miraculous moment never came.

Kramer felt he had been given a second chance; because of Lance, the childhood pain had finally lost its sting.

When they heard the front door open, Kramer and his wife both tensed. Lance strode into the living room then halted mid step, startled to find both of his parents sitting together on the sofa, looking up at him. He dropped his worn canvas book bag on an armchair.

"What's going on?"

"Lance -- we'd like to talk to you," Kramer said.

His son stood in the middle of the room, a questioning look on his face.

Kramer hesitated, and then pushed himself to say, "Your mother found something that concerned her. We're both concerned."

"Well?"

"She was putting some clothes in your bureau drawer. I think you know what she found."

"What do you mean?"

"She found several silver ornaments. Torah ornaments."

Silence.

"How did they get into your drawer?"

"I don't have to explain anything," Lance said, his eyes flashing. "It's none of your business. Besides, who said you could poke around in my drawer?"

"Nobody was poking around," Claire said. "When I put your underwear away the silver was there for everyone to see -- broad as daylight. And let's not have any of your smart talk." She paused to contain her anger, and then went on. "Now you tell us how you got those things."

"I said it's none of your business."

"Oh yeah? If there's stolen property in this house, it is my business." She turned to Kramer. "Let's call the police."

"Police?" Lance shouted. "What sort of shit is this? Are you crazy? I'll leave this place if you ever call the police!"

"Claire -- " Kramer reached out in a gesture of restraint. "Give him a chance. Let him talk."

"Okay." She turned to her son. "Talk."

"I don't want to talk."

He headed for the stairs, and his mother shouted, "Lance!"

Kramer pleaded, "Come on, Lance. Don't walk out on us -- this is important."

The boy hesitated at the foot of the staircase, and then turned to face his father.

"Tell us, Lance. How did those things get into your drawer?"

"Andy gave them to me."

"I see." He glanced at his wife, looking for a sign that perhaps she too might consider the possibility that Lance was not to blame after all. It could all be the fault of Andy, the boy they had urged Lance to avoid.

Kramer asked, "How did Andy get them?"

Lance shrugged.

"Come on, Lance. How did he get them?"

His son looked aside, hesitated, then said, "He stole them."

"From where?"

 "The Jewish synagogue."

"So Andy stole the ornaments and gave them to you?"

"Yeah."

"Why?"

"He asked me to keep the stuff until he was ready to sell it. He was afraid they'd find it on him in his house, so he asked me to hold it for him. He figured it would be safer here."

"I see. Well, I don't think that's a good idea, Lance. We can't keep stolen property in our house. We have to --"

"Is that all?" Claire demanded. "It's just a matter of getting rid of stolen property? Aren't you going to ask Lance what he had to do with all of this?"

"But he just told us it was Andy --"

"I can't believe it! How can you sit there and defend Lance when it's so obvious that he's involved?"

14

"Now wait a minute. I'm not going to jump on him and assume he's guilty. Let's be fair and give him a chance --"

Claire turned quickly to her son. "Tell us, Lance."

Lance shrugged, looking disgusted. "What do you want me to tell you? I said Andy asked me to keep the stuff."

"How did he get it?"

"Jeez... I told you. He stole it from the synagogue."

"How did he steal it?"

"Whaddaya mean, 'How'? He broke in at night."

"Were you with him?"

Lance hesitated and Kramer felt a sharp chill of anxiety. Perhaps noticing the change, his son was now looking at him.

"Yeah," Lance said slowly. "I was with him."

"You and Andy did it together," Kramer said.

"Yeah."

"Tell us about it."

"Well, we broke in two days ago, at night. You and Mom were asleep. I met Andy at the place -- he had the tools. We got inside and took the silver out of the closet where they keep those rolled up bibles. We saw what it was like on a television show about a kid's bar-mitzvah."

Kramer paused, thinking of his own bar-mitzvah. He remembered wearing his new blue serge suit and a blue and white prayer shawl. Two synagogue elders removed the silver-crowned Torahs from the open Holy Ark, then carefully rested one of the scrolls on the red-velvet covered reading table. When the cantor called out his name in ringing tones, the congregation was suddenly quiet, all eyes upon him as he stepped forward and stood with the elders at the table. He sang the blessings; the proper place in the open scroll before him was indicated with the pointer, and he chanted the Hebrew biblical passage he had prepared for that day. The Rabbi, his father, was standing at his side.

Claire's strident questioning drew him back. She was asking Lance, "Why? Why did you do it?"

15

Their son was silent.

"You've got to tell us," Kramer said. "If we can, we want to help you, but we have to know what this is all about."

"It was to get money. To sell the stuff and buy a car."

"A car?"

"Yeah. I was supposed to get a car on my birthday when I was sixteen, remember?"

He paused to let the sarcasm sink in. "Then you said I couldn't have a car because of my grades. So we decided to pick one up in time for my birthday. But then we realized we couldn't hide a car in this town so we stole the stuff to get enough money to buy one."

Claire's voice was subdued, "I think we should call the police." Seeing the consternation on his son's face, Kramer rested his hand on his wife's arm.

"Wait, Claire." Then he turned to Lance. "Was there anything else taken besides the ornaments?"

"No."

"Then everything is in your drawer?"

"Yeah, everything except the crown."

"What crown?" Claire asked.

"A big silver crown, Andy wanted to keep it."

Claire shook her head. "This is too much. The police will know all about it soon enough, if they don't already. They'll track down Andy -- and Lance. We should contact them now -- maybe through a lawyer. If there's an immediate confession, it'll go easier for everyone."

Lance shouted, "Andy will murder me!"

Kramer rose to calm his son, but Lance pulled away.

"Shit. I'm getting out of here. I'm not hanging around, waiting for the cops!"

He turned and ran up the stairs, his mother calling after him, "Lance!" They heard him slam his bedroom door.

"We can't call the police," Kramer said.

"What should we do?"

"We'll return the ornaments -- give them back."

"How? At night, with another break in? By Lance and Andy? Or do we the parents just wrap up everything and leave it in the lobby, like a baby abandoned in a church?"

Kramer, silent, again saw his son staring at him from behind bars.

Claire's voice was now insistent. "I think we should contact the police. If Lance gets away with this, he'll do something worse next time. He's got to face the consequences of his behavior."

"Claire, you're talking about the juvenile detention center. Prison. Is that what you want for your son?"

"Of course not! But this has been going on for years! When he's been in trouble before we always covered up for him. He's gotten everything he ever wanted -- expensive bikes, sports equipment, stereos, and all those skateboards -- the best. We've spoiled him, don't you see it? You're a psychologist, for heaven's sake ..."

It was the closest she had come to blaming him. All along she had been saying "we," never "you," but the accusation was there, he felt its edge below the surface of her anger. He was the one who had spoiled, overindulged. She was the one to sound warnings, after each theft, each school failure, each fight, each truancy.

For years she had demanded that they do something, that he apply his psychological knowledge. Wasn't he the authority, the consultant to schools and institutions? Hadn't he published all those papers?

"You're the expert," she would say. "What if it wasn't your son but some other boy, what would you do?"

In response to her urging in the past, he had devised programs based on the principles of operant conditioning -- reinforcement schedules -- programs that worked for a while, and then fizzled out. The last disaster was the car. Had Lance gotten a passing grade in at least three subjects, he would have earned the car and the synagogue theft would not have occurred.

"You're right," Kramer said. "I've spoiled him. I accept the blame. But jail? I couldn't bear sending him to jail. I want to give him another chance."

"But we're getting into serious crime now -- if we don't stop it here, we're just encouraging more! It may already be too late --"

"I don't want my son to go to jail."

"If he confesses before they come after him, maybe it won't be jail," Claire said.

"And even if he's put away for a while, it might be good for him -- in the long run."

"How can you say that? We've already lost one child -- do you want to lose him too?"

Claire began to cry softly and he regretted at once what he had said. "I'm sorry."

When the crying didn't stop, he put his arm about her shoulders, drawing her closer, feeling pity for her, anger at himself.

"Claire -- I'm sorry."

Not looking at him, she sat limp and unresisting in his embrace, as though he weren't there. He waited, and the crying eventually trailed off into a pained whimper.

Finally she said in a hushed voice, "Please Dan. Don't destroy us."

He was quiet for a while, and then said, "I'm not calling the police. I just can't do that to him. But I won't yield to Lance again. I promise." Then he added, "I'll return the ornaments."

She looked up. "How?"

"I'll contact the rabbi. I'll ask him if I can return the ornaments. I won't reveal who took them."

The crying stopped.

"It shouldn't be too difficult," Kramer said. "I know the rabbi."

"You know him?"

"Yes. His name is Himmelshine." Kramer paused under the weight of memory. "We went to school together."

Chapter 4

Kramer looked up the phone number and called.

"This is Professor Kramer," he said. "I'd like to see Rabbi Himmelshine. It's a matter of some urgency."

The woman who answered hesitated, and then asked, "Urgency?"

"It's about my son."

"Oh."

He was given an appointment for the following day.

So many years had passed since their last, painful encounter. Once fellow rabbinical students, Kramer had become a different person. He wondered if Himmelshine would remember.

Arriving early, Kramer entered the synagogue lobby; it was quiet and empty. A display case of ceremonial objects caught his attention: antique and contemporary mezuzot, wine goblets, filigree spice boxes and a pair of heavy silver old-world Sabbath candlesticks. On one lobby wall there was an honor roll of donors to the building fund; on the other, small bronze memorial plaques bearing the names of members who had died. Alongside two of the plaques a miniature electric bulb radiated a soft glow, commemorating the anniversary of death. Kramer thought of his parents; there was no memorial for them other than the tombstone with its Hebrew and English inscription.

He glanced through the doors that led to the sanctuary, row upon row of seats, all empty, yet retaining the aura of absent worshipers. Kramer looked down the center aisle toward the Holy Ark, its door covered by a gold-embroidered curtain. Above the Holy Ark was an engraved replica of the Ten Commandments, guarded on each side by a carved golden lion, sentinels that had failed to protect the Holy Ark from his son. Kramer contemplated the spot where Lance must have stood -- the place of his son's chance encounter with his ancestral past. Finally turning away, Kramer found a sign pointing to the office.

"I have an appointment with Rabbi Himmelshine," he said to the woman at the desk.

"Professor Kramer?"

"Yes."

She phoned that he had arrived, and then gave him directions to the Rabbi's study. As he approached the open door he could see bookshelves lining a wall, holding tall volumes of the Talmud as well as an array of books and paperbacks. Where the wall held no books, the space was taken by framed photographs, diplomas and certificates. Himmelshine was seated behind a large, paper-cluttered desk.

The bright red hair was much thinner than Kramer remembered, and flecked with gray; the pudgy face was now lined and bejowled but the gap-toothed smile was the same.

As Himmelshine rose and extended his hand, Kramer realized that his old schoolmate did not recognize him. With a momentary twinge, Kramer wondered if age had so dramatically changed his appearance; then it occurred to him that his beard now masked his identity.

"Thank you for seeing me, Rabbi." He paused, then said, "I learned about a recent theft -- here, at your synagogue."

Himmelshine raised his eyebrows. "A theft?"

"Yes."

"What do you mean?"

"Torah ornaments. They were stolen from your synagogue. You didn't know?"

"What are you talking about?"

"Two days ago silver Torah ornaments were stolen from the aron kodesh."

Himmelshine stared at him, and then rose quickly. "Let's go and look." He followed Himmelshine out of the study to the sanctuary.

Before heading down the aisle, Kramer reached into the box that held yarmulkes and put one on. Perched on the back of his head, it was an odd sensation from his past.

Himmelshine stood before the Holy Ark, drew open the curtain, then pulled aside the wooden doors, exposing several velvet covered Torah scrolls resting against the wall.

"They're gone! The crown, the breastplate, the rimonim, the yad ..." He turned to Kramer. "Where are they?"

Kramer hesitated. "I just learned of the theft."

"Yes, but what happened? Where are the ornaments?"

"I can arrange for their return."

Himmelshine closed the ark. "Let's go back to my study."

They walked in silence, Himmelshine grim, his short strides rapid. In the study he closed the door, then leaning forward, he faced Kramer across his desk.

"Now tell me. What's this all about? What's going on?"

It was an echo of the confrontation that ended their friendship. Himmelshine asked the questions this time, staring at Kramer, waiting for a reply.

"It's my son."

Kramer paused, trying to keep an unexpected surge of feeling under control. "He's seventeen––a good boy, basically, but under the influence of an undesirable friend. The two of them––they entered your synagogue through a window two nights ago and stole the ornaments."

"Where are the ornaments now?"

"My wife found them hidden in my son's bureau drawer while she was putting away some underwear. He admitted the break-in. His friend is on probation with a police record. He told our boy to hide the ornaments in our house until they could be sold.

Irritation in his voice, Himmelshine asked again, "Where are they?"

"I have them. I'll return them today. I wanted to speak to you first."

"Get them. I'll wait."

"I have a class. How about later today? This evening, after dinner?"

"Seven o'clock. I'll be here."

Carrying the shopping bag containing the ornaments into the synagogue seemed surreptitious and Kramer was relieved not to be seen by anyone. Himmelshine took the bag and carefully laid out its contents on his desk, examining each piece. Then he looked up at Kramer.

"The crown is missing."

"Andy -- the other boy -- has it. I'll get it from him."

"When?"

"Tomorrow, I'll ask Lance where Andy lives, and I'll go there," Kramer said. "I'll bring you the crown tomorrow."

<u>Chapter 5</u>

Andy's street was unfamiliar to him; he finally located it on the county map he kept in the glove compartment of his car. He drove past a few deserted factories with broken windows, then a freight yard with several truck trailers lined up near a terminal building. With his map on the seat beside him, Kramer located the street; it held small frame houses, the paint on most of them faded or peeling.

He found the house. A wooden beam, placed at an angle, buttressed a corner of the sagging porch ceiling. Patches of uncut grass were in the small plot in front of the house.

Kramer made his way cautiously up the wooden steps to the porch, empty except for an old glider with torn cushions and a rusting frame. He rang the bell but nothing happened. Instead of ringing again, he knocked loudly. Soon he heard muffled sounds and the door creaked open, only wide enough for a gray-haired woman in a shapeless lavender housecoat to peer out.

"I'm looking for Andy -- is he in?"

The woman hesitated, and then opened the door fully. "He's in his room upstairs, on the right."

Kramer headed for the staircase through a dark living room with drawn shades, catching a glimpse of an old fashioned kitchen in the rear with a sink full of dishes.

The house had a wet basement smell. He grasped the banister and made his way up the worn uncarpeted stairs.

The sound of rock music came through the closed door; Kramer knocked and someone called out, "Come in."

He opened the door and saw a girl in her late teens sitting on an unmade bed. Her hair was uncombed, and her wide face and coarse features conveyed the appearance of mental dullness. She was holding a lighted cigarette. In a corner of the room facing her, Andy sat in an easy chair that listed to the side, his feet up on a torn hassock. The two of them looked at Kramer with silent surprise, and then the girl took a drag on her cigarette.

She wore a frayed blue chenille robe. As she leaned over to flick an ash into a butt-filled plate on the floor, the top of her robe opened, exposing one of her breasts.

"Hello there," Andy said in a mock comic voice. As he reached over to turn down the sound on the boom box beside his chair, Kramer saw a tattoo of the Nazi flag on his thin arm.

Andy pointed to the girl. "That's my sister Essie."

The girl looked at him, her face devoid of emotion. Kramer nodded, then said to Andy, "I'd like to talk to you."

"Sure."

"Can we talk alone?"

"You can talk here," Andy said.

The girl, staring at Kramer, took another drag on her cigarette. Andy said, "Go ahead."

Kramer tried to focus on Andy but found it difficult to shift his attention from the girl. Finally he turned away from her.

"It's about the ornaments you and Lance took from the synagogue." Kramer added quickly, "Lance didn't come to us about it. We found the things hidden in his drawer."

"Yeah, I know."

"Lance told you?"

"Yeah." Andy grinned. "I was expecting you."

The mocking tone, the knowing smile, the stained teeth were all oddly familiar, resonating old anxieties; in a flash of memory Kramer saw forgotten bullies from his childhood.

He paused, and then said, "I'm here for the crown."

"The crown?"

"Yes."

Andy looked away for a few moments of silent thought, then said, "I like that crown."

After pausing for more thought, Andy got up and opened the closet door; reaching for a pile of clothing on the shelf, he withdrew the crown, large and ornate in its silver glory. Andy held the crown, studying it, seemingly reluctant to yield it, and as Kramer waited he was struck by the contrast -- an object of beauty and holiness held in contemplative admiration by this thin, unkempt, tattooed boy.

At last Andy handed him the crown. "Maybe I'll get it back some day," he said with a smile.

The encounter with Andy left an unpleasant, lingering aftertaste as Kramer drove home, the crown locked safely in the trunk.

After calling the following morning to make sure that Himmelshine would be there, Kramer arrived at the synagogue and carried a paper shopping bag into the rabbi's office. Reaching into the bag, Himmelshine pulled out the crown, examined it, and then turned to Kramer.

"Looks fine," he said. "Thank you."

Kramer turned to leave.

"Wait a minute."

Kramer stopped at the office door.

"This isn't over."

PART TWO
Chapter 6

When they had first met, it didn't occur to Kramer that the short, pudgy man with the unwieldy mop of red hair was, like himself, a student at the rabbinical college. It was Kramer's first day at the school. Shortly after his arrival by cab he located his dormitory room then closed the door and left, his trunk sent earlier still in the middle of the floor, unopened. It was almost time for lunch and he didn't want to be late. Walking down the unfamiliar hall, he took the elevator to the lounge where students were beginning to gather. As Kramer headed for the dining room, a short man wearing a baggy suit turned to him and extended a fat hand.

"I'm Himmelshine," he announced, his smile displaying teeth that were widely spaced.

Kramer shook hands, gave his name and asked, "Do you work here?"

"Rarely," Himmelshine said, flashing his gap-toothed smile.

As they made their way to the dining room, Himmelshine remained at his side, pausing to introduce him to other students, and Kramer realized that his companion was an upperclassman. Under Himmelshine's guidance, Kramer helped himself to a plastic tray and stood in line at the serving counter. With grand flourishes of his short arms,

Himmelshine provided an orientation to the new setting. "Here you will find the silverware -- napkins -- there is the bread -- you can choose coffee, tea or milk."

There were introductions to the white-jacketed staff ladling out food, to the dining room manager hovering in the background, and then to the cashier, an elderly woman who punched the meal tickets.

"A new student," Himmelshine announced, as though he were an impresario and Kramer a star performer.

They took their trays to a table, and Himmelshine reminded Kramer that the rabbinical school provided food as well as lodgings at no cost to the students.

"Yes, we're all on scholarships here. No earthly concerns to keep us from total dedication to Torah." He finished his soup and patted his lips with a napkin.

Kramer asked, "How is it possible for all of us to receive scholarships?"

"A generous benefactor. Years ago, a noble merchant prince named Joshua Pleet endowed the student body with perpetual feed and a place to sleep. Pleet was a man of humble origins who rose to great wealth -- he knew how an empty stomach could distract one from scholarly pursuits." Himmelshine paused, his voice solemn. "I wrote a poem in honor of our benefactor. Would you like to hear it?"

Kramer felt he had to say yes, and Himmelshine intoned, "Forever indebted to Joshua Pleet

For our daily portion of bread and meat

Young rabbis devour his posthumous salary

Of bed, board, Cabala and calorie."

Kramer was amused, but only for a moment. He was quite serious about his vocation then and felt a mild aversion toward Himmelshine and his humor. Had Himmelshine forgotten the impoverished rabbinical students of the past, whose beds were the hard benches of the yeshiva, and who found relief from hunger only on the Sabbath, if fortunate enough to be invited to someone's home? And further back in time, what of the grim privations endured by Hillel, Akiba and other sages in their passion to study Torah -- was not Himmelshine mocking them all?

For the remainder of the meal, Kramer said little. But when they left the dining room, he felt courtesy required a parting comment. "I guess I'll see you tomorrow morning at services."

Himmelshine shook his head. "I won't be there. Prayer is verbal masturbation. I haven't prayed since God knows when."

Kramer immersed himself in the study of Talmud, Bible and Jewish history, and made new friends. But although he succeeded in avoiding Himmelshine, he could not escape the impact of

Himmelshine's irreverent views. Kramer found himself questioning ideas and beliefs that he had always taken for granted. He now examined more closely his daily prayers with their recital of God's attributes -- merciful, loving, and forgiving. Especially disturbing was the expression of God's great love for His people. How could Jews continue to believe in a just and loving God in the face of their horrific history? And how could he become a rabbi who would lead others in the worship of this God?

At night his ruminations kept him awake. He spent hours in the school library searching through classic texts yet failed to discover satisfactory answers. He was reluctant to approach his professors, fearing they would ridicule his concerns as being naive, or worse, that they might admit to equally heretical views.

He finally decided to discuss his doubts with his father. Their relationship had always been a good one; perhaps that was one of the reasons he had chosen to follow his father's career. European born, with a neatly trimmed gray-black beard, his father was an Orthodox rabbi. Kramer felt he could be open with his soft-spoken, accepting father; perhaps the older man with his maturity would point to some intellectual resolution -- a sort of updating of Maimonides' "Guide for the Perplexed." Kramer told himself that there might be flaws in his own thinking, acceptable rationalizations that he had overlooked.

It was on a visit home months later that Kramer had an opportunity to bring up the matter. He and his father were returning from the synagogue after an early morning weekday service, past the line of stores that had not yet opened for the day -- the Jewish bakery, the delicatessen with Hebrew National salamis hanging in the widow, the kosher butcher shop. The street was silent, the fragrance of the spring air not yet fouled by traffic exhaust. It was like the days of his adolescence, but the morning walks then had been free of doubts and self-questioning.

"Dad," he said. His father glanced up at him, and he realized he didn't know how to begin. "I've been doing a lot of thinking," he said. "I've been going through some conflict about becoming a rabbi."

"Is that so?" His father's tone was one of support rather than surprise.

"The idea of God and Jewish suffering -- I find it more difficult these days."

"More difficult?"

"It's strange. Now that I've been at rabbinical school for almost a year, you'd think I'd be more committed to Judaism, what with the greater focus, all the study Talmud, the Prophets, ritual. But instead, I've developed doubts I've never had before."

His father nodded, and Kramer went on. "I've become preoccupied with the Holocaust -- not just with the terrible events and the books and films. It's the religious implications. Where was God during the Holocaust? We say in our daily prayers that God has a great love for us, His people -- what kind of love did God show during the slaughter of millions?"

There was a catch in his voice and Kramer stopped talking, surprised at the wave. "It's pretty upsetting," Kramer said. "We pray to God every day, we praise His power, His goodness, His love for us. We sing that the Torah is 'A tree of life for all who grasp it. 'A tree of life?' Isn't that a mockery?"

His father sighed, and then said in his faintly accented voice, "You ask important questions. Others have asked the same questions."

"Well -- is there an answer? How can Jews believe in a God that loves them, that has chosen them from among all other peoples? How can we repeat this in prayers every day -- how could I, as a rabbi, honestly lead others in such prayers, in the face of what has happened?"

His father paused, and then said, "You are right, of course. God did turn his face away from his people. Why? Rabbis, wise men, have tried to answer this question. I personally haven't found an answer that makes sense. It's a question that has no answer. There are such questions. Maybe someday there will be an answer. Things happen that we can't predict -- who would have believed that an airplane could be invented? Or that sound waves, and viruses, would be discovered? That a Jewish state would be reestablished in our time? Perhaps, someday, there will be an answer to your question. Until then, we live by faith, by tradition. We have our past -- God gave Moses the Torah, we have Israel -- we must thank God for the good things."

It was difficult for Kramer to accept such a philosophy, but he did not tell his father this. He was grateful that the answer to his question was not the deplorable one given by some extremist rabbis who, in their effort to reconcile the view of a perfect and compassionate God with the horrors of the Holocaust, concluded that the victims must have been punished for their sins.

He saw no point in pushing the argument; his father had his own life -- it was already set, fixed. But he, Dan Kramer, was just beginning a career, one that now gave him serious doubts. He still had time to change his direction.

"We must have hope," his father added. "What would happen if we had no hope? If we gave up our religion, our identity? The Jewish People would eventually disappear, like the others -- the Edomites, the Philistines, the Romans. We must hold on to the Torah, this is what has sustained us, this is our life and the length of our days..."

His father walked beside him with his familiar methodical gait, wearing his black Homburg hat and dark suit; a dignified man, usually restrained in his expression of feeling. But now his voice had risen, and Kramer remained silent, not wishing to add some contentious note that might spoil the quiet pleasure of the early morning walk. He had always thought of his father as the controlled, decorous parent; it was his mother who was the emotional one, more open, freer in spirit.

While committed to the standards of Jewish tradition, at times she would permit deviations, in the service of some esthetic ideal. He recalled her Saturday afternoon ritual of surreptitious listening to the radio, a prohibited activity, to hear the weekly broadcast of the Metropolitan Opera, announced by Milton Cross whom she adored; she listened bent over, close to the radio, the volume low, not to awaken his father from his Sabbath nap.

It was to her that he confided his conflict in greater detail. "I may have to quit rabbinical school and start a new life."

Chapter 7

His attendance at morning services in the rabbinical college synagogue, which had become erratic, now ceased completely, and he began to move away from other religious observances as well.

A lifetime of dedication to Jewish tradition was crumbling, shaken by doubts he could no longer resolve. He began to experiment with non-Kosher foods; first, a furtive order of scrambled eggs at a drug store lunch counter -- eggs prepared in the same black skillet where strips of bacon had crackled earlier. Then he had a lamb chop dinner in a restaurant a safe distance from the rabbinical school. Next it was a bacon, lettuce and tomato sandwich.

Not attending morning services meant sleeping later, at times missing breakfast in the school dining room. One late morning he walked several blocks to a restaurant he had not tried before, and took a table in the rear. After looking about to make certain he didn't know any of the other patrons, he whispered his order to the waitress, a pretty young woman who had to bend down to hear him. Just as she returned with his bacon and eggs, he was horrified to see Himmelshine walk in the front door. Himmelshine spotted Kramer at once, his round pink face breaking into a wide grin.

"Aha!" he said. "So you too are a late riser!"

Not waiting for an invitation, Himmelshine pulled up a chair and Kramer watched him with anxiety, waiting for some response to the platter on the table. The waitress appeared and gave Himmelshine a bright smile of recognition. "The usual, my dear," he said.

When the waitress left, Kramer asked Himmelshine if he knew her.

"Yes indeed. Her name is Flora." With his toothy grin, he added as an afterthought, "I've had a lot of fauna with Flora."

Soon Flora returned with a loaded tray of orange juice, toast, ham and eggs, potatoes and coffee, and Himmelshine explained, "I like a substantial breakfast -- you just can't get this in our dining room."

After breakfast Kramer agreed that the crisp April day should not be spent in class; they took a bus to Washington Square. In evenings that followed they made the rounds together –- dances at Columbia and NYU, bars in the Village. The pattern quickly emerged: Himmelshine charmed the girls and soon he went off with one of them, leaving Kramer behind, alone.

"You're too intellectual, too serious," he'd say. "You're putting Descartes before the horse. Save the philosophy for later."

Kramer found the dishonesty of his double life increasingly difficult to tolerate; he spent hours in the Forty-Second Street library reading about alternative careers but was unable to make a choice. He had hoped to leave rabbinical school by summer at the latest, but found himself back again in the fall, uncertain and undecided. The arrival of the High Holidays precipitated a crisis.

He was assigned to officiate at one of the small, isolated communities that had no rabbi during the year, but hired a rabbinical student for Rosh Hashanah and Yom Kippur. After much conflict, he concluded that it would be morally unacceptable to preach before his as yet unseen congregation. He decided to cancel the trip.

Himmelshine tried to dissuade him. "A commitment has been made to those people. You can't pull out now."

Kramer insisted that the greater commitment was to be honest with the congregation he was due to serve. "I no longer believe prayer has any meaning," he said. "How can I tell Jews that God loves them?"

"Stop being a philosopher," Himmelshine insisted. "You've never conducted a service before. Go to your congregation, see what it's like, and then draw your conclusions. Must you believe everything you say? So what if you sell poetic illusions -- isn't every role a deception? Who is really himself when he earns his livelihood? Everyone tries to be what the boss, the client, the customer, the patient, expects him to be. Every role is a mask; the

33

difference between people is that some realize they are actors, others don't. I know I'm an actor. In this world of deceivers, my boy, the only real deception is self-deception."

Kramer found himself relenting. He agreed that since he had never officiated at a service it was unreasonable not to give it a try. He would be meeting his obligation, as well as testing his decision to leave the school.

Himmelshine shook his head in mock exasperation. Looking up, he raised his hands heavenward and asked, "Why do people insist on making a moral issue out of religion?"

With Himmelshine's support, Kramer was able to suppress concerns about honesty. He completed preparations for the trip to the South Carolina community where he was to spend the High Holidays, but then developed a new fear.

The night before his departure, he dreamed that it was the eve of the Day of Atonement. He was in an old Orthodox synagogue, with cream-colored walls that had long turned dark yellow, heavy mahogany woodwork, and a women's balcony that faded into the shadows.

The worship was led by his grandfather, a tall, white-bearded man of awesome piety. He was chanting the Kol Nidre before the open Holy Ark. Kramer was standing beside him, peering beyond the Torahs into the recesses of the ark, which in childhood he believed contained a hidden passageway to God. On this most sacred night of the year Kramer was surprised to find a small brown paper bag in his hand; he opened the bag and extracted a sandwich. The praying halted in abrupt silence, and to everyone's horror, including his own, Kramer unwrapped the sandwich, raised it to his mouth, and violating the fast, took a bite.

His grandfather's voice pierced the tense stillness with a scream; the old man lunged at his grandson and tried to snatch the sandwich away, but Kramer held on to it and managed another bite. Several worshipers leaped onto the platform in front of the open ark, joining his grandfather in the struggle. Soon Kramer was on the floor, caught up in a tangle of prayer shawls and fringes; then somehow he managed to pull himself free. Bounding off of the platform, sandwich in hand, Kramer raced to the synagogue exit; he made it safely to the street, and after running for some time slowed his pace, gasping.

He happened to glance over his shoulder and was shocked to see the entire congregation in hot pursuit, the men in the lead with their prayer shawls fluttering in the wind, the women and children close behind. Gripped by fear, he resumed his flight with redoubled effort. Yet the congregation kept drawing closer, and when finally a wild-eyed man in the lead reached out to grab him he awoke, heart pounding, his forehead damp with perspiration.

As he lay in bed recovering, wide awake, Kramer wondered if the dream was a warning. He would be going to South Carolina as an impostor; perhaps, as in the dream, his hypocrisy would erupt in a scandalous involuntary act -- a return of the repressed. The congregation, in righteous anger at being deceived, would then turn its fury upon him.

This dread dominated his consciousness throughout the High Holidays -- during the prayers, his sermons, and the strained visits to the homes of his congregants. Until the last moment, while being driven to the airport for the return trip home, he was on the alert to possible disaster. None occurred.

When he described the experience, Himmelshine said, "See? God was with you despite your lost faith."

The trip confirmed Kramer's decision; he informed Himmelshine that he was quitting rabbinical school. Had he left at once, he and Himmelshine might have remained friends.

Chapter 8

He delayed his departure because he had no alternative plan. Where would he go? What would he do? He didn't want to move back home to dependence upon his parents. He had to find a new direction for his life, and that required thought, exploration and time.

A woman was the second reason for staying on a while longer. Annamarie had come from Bavaria to study the harpsichord at Julliard. She was a wispy creature who wore her dark hair in a bun; her accented English was subdued and halting. She wished to convert to Judaism, and Kramer was asked to be her tutor in Hebrew, Jewish history, and religion. He knew he was the wrong person for the job, but his reluctance dissolved when he saw her for the first time.

Curiosity as well as attraction drew him to him to her. Why was she embracing the Jewish faith? He asked her directly during a history lesson one gloomy November afternoon, when they were reviewing the slaughter of Jewish communities in Europe by the crusaders on their way to rescue the Holy Land.

"Why do you want to take on this pain?"

Her dark eyes flashed and Kramer was taken aback by her vehemence.

"I must!"

Later he learned that her decision to convert was prompted by guilt over the fate of the Jews of Europe. In particular, the deportation of her closest friend, a Jewish girl her own age, continued to haunt her. "They came and took her away --we were playing on the rug in her parlor with our dolls."

Annamarie made rapid progress in her studies, but as they sat together Kramer was unable to keep his attention on the open texts before them. There were moments of silence that ended only when her glance made him realize he had been staring at her. She was aware of his infatuation long before he was; her response was one of amused but kindly tolerance.

At first, Himmelshine teased Kramer about his preoccupation with Annamarie, for he now spoke of nothing else. However, when Kramer confided that he wanted to marry her, Himmelshine grew serious and refused to comment.

"The humble man sticks to his area of competence," he explained. "I can tell you all you wish to know about God, but don't ask me about love."

At last Kramer summoned up the courage to reveal his feelings to his student. She phoned him one morning before breakfast to say that she couldn't come for her lesson because of illness. Standing in the hall telephone booth in his bathrobe, Kramer offered to go to her home. She hesitated, then with much gratitude, accepted.

She lived with a relative, a woman psychiatrist who had offices and an apartment in a town house on Sutton Place. As Kramer stood at the front door he could hear the rhythms of a Scarlatti sonata. A uniformed maid let him in and directed him to a spacious, high ceiling Victorian living room where he found Annamarie at the harpsichord beside a tall red-draped window. Kramer stood still at the room entrance, and when Annamarie stopped playing he remained silent.

She asked, "Is everything all right?"

He nodded, and they sat down side by side at the small antique table that held her books. She looked at him, waiting, but instead of describing the lesson of the day as he always did, he told her that there was something he had to say:

"Annamarie..."

She seemed puzzled by his hesitation. He finally blurted out, "Annamarie, I care for you a great deal."

Her smile faded.

"I am so sorry."

Gently she said that while very fond of him, there was someone else.

Suddenly flooded by a heavy melancholy, Kramer could not speak. At last Annamarie broke the silence by picking up her prayer book and stumbling through a Hebrew passage.

In the dreary days that followed, he took long walks along Riverside Drive, tormenting himself with the fantasy that her boyfriend was probably a music student too, perhaps a violinist with whom she played Bach sonatas. Kramer could see them standing on a stage together, bowing before an enthusiastic, applauding audience. The scene would take place in the baroque hall of some foreign city, a venue like the La Scala, for soon they would go on concert tours throughout the world.

It was too painful to continue the lessons, and Kramer wrote a letter to Annamarie, terminating their arrangement. But this did not end his consuming preoccupation. Soon he was berating himself for having cut off the possibility of ever seeing her again. The desire to look at her one more time grew overwhelming, and one warm April day after class he went to her house, posted himself unobtrusively across the street and waited for her appearance. The hours seemed endless; streams of cars, trucks, and people passed; then at dusk a cab drew up. The door swung open and Annamarie, laughing, stepped out with her escort. It was Himmelshine. They walked hand in hand to her house and soon were gone.

Kramer managed to get back to the school dormitory; he found a spot in the lounge near the elevator and waited. It was well after midnight when he heard the sound of distant footsteps on the concrete floor. The sound grew louder and then Himmelshine appeared; his seersucker jacket over his arm, his tie pulled loose at an open collar. He stopped suddenly when he saw Kramer. He smiled the old, familiar, wide-spaced smile, but the twinkle in his eyes was missing.

Kramer rose, his sadness swept away by fury.

"Why did you do it?"

Himmelshine pulled back, startled, and his paunch, hanging over the edge of his belt, seemed about to break out of his shirt. Kramer punched him with a hard blow to the belly; uttering a grunt, Himmelshine fell back into a leather armchair.

"You knew how I felt about her." Kramer's tremulous voice echoed through the empty lounge. "I thought you were my friend."

Himmelshine raised an arm in a protective gesture as Kramer stood over him.

"You're not my friend," Kramer said. "You're my enemy."

Himmelshine looked up and tried to smile. "I am both," he said. "Isn't every man?"

Chapter 9

He hoped he would never see Himmelshine again, and after their encounter Kramer knew it was time to leave the rabbinical college. He wanted to go quietly, without fellow students asking why. He began packing that night. Squeezing as much of his clothing as possible into his trunk, he went on to fill his suitcase. He surveyed the books waiting to be packed and realized he didn't have enough room. He'd leave much behind, and the effort took far longer than he had anticipated.

It was after two o'clock. Fatigued by the unaccustomed exertion, he sat down to rest. He listened to the night silence of the dormitory and was engulfed by a wave of sadness; soon he would slip away unseen, never again to be a part of the place and people who had been his life.

He hoped to finish packing that night; it now occurred to him that there might be some boxes in the basement. Quietly opening the door to his room, he peered down the dimly lit hall. A mute emptiness had replaced the people and voices of the day. He tried to soften the sound of his footsteps as he walked past closed doors and silent rooms. He pressed the button for the elevator. Inaudible during the day, it now rumbled up to his floor like a train rolling into a station.

He'd never been to the basement before, and when the elevator door slid open he faced darkness and a haunting silence. He eventually found the light switch; a maze of overhead pipes and ducts, several storage bins and a giant furnace sprang into view. Searching for boxes, he felt like an interloper, a thief in the night. In a corner, he found three empty cartons.

He managed to get the boxes up to his room, and as he filled them old images returned -- scenes that always flooded his mind when he packed, or walked by a luggage store, or saw a traveler with a suitcase: scenes of a family, unknown yet somehow familiar, one of the many families that had arisen early, hurrying to complete packing in a cloud of anxiety; father and mother making hopeless attempts to reassure frightened children and cope their own dread, struggling to decide which few items to pack, unaware that their efforts were futile, that they would never see the carefully folded clothing again. Suitcase in hand, they would join all the others in the street, silent but for the sound of countless feet trudging, a human river moving toward the collection point for a journey to the abyss.

It was past three o'clock when the cartons were filled and sealed; heaped in a corner were items he had to leave behind. His chair, a stained second hand recliner he had bought in a used furniture store, would remain.

Standing before an open window, he wiped the sweat from his face with a towel, and then cleaned his glasses with his handkerchief. The night air failed to cool him. He looked down through the dark at the grassy field that lay behind the dormitory building; in a few weeks it would be crowded and festive in the afternoon sun. He saw robed faculty and students, guests seated on rows of folding chairs, and then the solemn commencement procession. He would never be there.

But this was not for him, and he was suddenly energized by the knowledge that he was being true to himself. His heart beat more rapidly as he attached notes to the trunk and boxes explaining that they would be picked up by Railway Express. Then he wrote a letter to the dean stating that he was withdrawing from the school.

At the door, he paused to glance at the trunk and boxes in the room that was now bare, stripped of its identity. Other students had lived in the room before him; new students would move in, replacing him. Rooms were like people, he thought; each has a life that grows, flourishes, then dies, to be resurrected by the arrival of a new occupant.

He stepped out of his room into the silent hall and quietly closed the door.

Kramer walked up the familiar front steps.

"Danny!"

His mother came forward from the kitchen, wiping her hands on her apron.

"Are you all right?"

"I'm fine." He put down his suitcase and kissed her on the cheek.

"What a surprise! I thought it was your father, coming home from shul!"

He could see his father walking home from morning prayers along the familiar route they had taken together so many times in the past.

His mother stepped back, looking at him; it was the usual inspection after a period of separation, a rapid visual check to determine if all was well.

"So tell me, why the sudden visit?" She hastened to correct a possible implication that he was unwelcome. "Of course, it's wonderful to see you --

"Mom, I quit."

"Quit?"

"I left the rabbinical college."

Her face was suddenly drawn. She stood still for a moment, looking at him, and then nodded as she headed for the sofa.

"I see."

"I decided it wasn't for me. It would be a mistake if I continued -- it would be wrong."

He had hinted about his doubts and misgivings before, yet he saw that she was taken aback. Her silence was broken by the sound of the door being unlocked; his father came into the room and exclaimed, "Well well! A guest!"

Unlike his mother's look of concern upon his arrival, his father was smiling with pleasure. He extended his hand. "What a surprise!"

He removed the familiar black Homburg then turned to his son. "And to what do we owe this unexpected visit?"

"Dad -- you and I talked about my concerns -- about being a rabbi. Well -- I've decided not to continue. I've left the rabbinical college."

His father lowered his head in silent reflection, and after a few moments looked up.

"Maybe you should ask for a leave of absence. So you could take some time to give it more thought."

Kramer shook his head. "I've given it a lot of thought. It's not a sudden decision."

"Have you talked to someone about this, maybe one of your professors?"

"No. Well, I did go over it with a classmate." He didn't want to say Himmelshine was a friend. "But it's something I've had to work out by myself."

Again his father was silent, looking down at the floor, deep in thought. Then he asked, "What are you going to do?"

His mother leaned forward to catch his reply. He hesitated, and then said, "I don't know."

Chapter 10

It felt odd, living at home again. At first he thought the feeling was temporary, a consequence of the transition in his life. Soon he would have a comfortable, easy-going relationship with his parents, as in the past.

The first few days he slept late. He realized that his conflict and the resulting life change had drained him; he needed time for recovery. Yet he was preoccupied with the image of his father walking alone, without him, to the daily morning service. Soon he would join his father as he did in the past. It would not be hypocrisy because he was extending himself to please a parent. Honor thy father and thy mother. On Saturday, he would definitely get up early and go with his father to Sabbath services. He set the alarm to make sure.

When the alarm went off and he quickly reached out to silence it, he lay in bed for a long time, unable to get up, realizing at last that he would never go with his father or anyone else to a synagogue service again.

His parents seemed to ignore the changes in his behavior. Sleeping late, not wearing his yarmulke during meals, skipping morning prayers -- all appeared to pass unnoticed. His father continued to be accepting, his mother caring. Yet he felt a tension in the air.

A routine had developed: late breakfast, then out to the back porch and warm spring sun to read the Philadelphia Inquirer and the Times over a second cup of coffee. It was a quiet time of day. He would glance up and down the row of small back yards, some with gardens beginning to blossom, and saw no one; the rest of the world was at work. The afternoons consisted of reading, casual and at times strained conversations with his parents, and perhaps a ride into center city for a visit to the art museum, the Franklin Institute, or a movie.

The tension at home seemed to be increasing; he sensed that his parents were growing concerned. His mother's face seemed drawn, his father's words more cautious. It was time to end the slide toward indolence and do something about his life.

Sleeping late gave way to early morning rising. Each day after breakfast he took the bus to the main branch of the library on the Benjamin Franklin Parkway. There he spent the day in the main reading room, researching a range of vocational possibilities -- law, journalism, education, social work, psychology, medicine.

It was a time of isolation. He hoped he wouldn't see anyone he knew and avoided calling old friends. The prospect of an encounter and the need to explain -- "I quit rabbinical school. I'm living at home...doing nothing right now. I haven't yet decided...."

It would be too awkward, this admission of being out of step with the rest of the world.

In the end, he decided upon an academic career. As an undergraduate, he discovered an unexpected pleasure in speaking before a class. And he felt drawn to a life of scholarship. He would go on with graduate work in his undergraduate major, psychology.

His mother seemed relieved and pleased; his father, offering wishes of good luck, conveyed a restraint that Kramer saw as disappointment. With his decision made, Kramer rushed applications to meet deadlines.

From among several acceptances he chose Teachers College at Columbia; the school offered him a graduate assistantship and the city was familiar. A week later, in the middle of a heat wave, he was back in Manhattan, looking for a cheap place to live, and in a rooming house near Second Avenue he found a furnished room whose single window looked out on a lone sumac tree in a tiny rear yard. His new life had begun.

Chapter 11

With his courses and the demands of his assistantship-- literature searches and summaries, hours spent interviewing subjects for his professor's research -- the pace was exhausting and there was never enough time. Kramer spent his nights in his room or in the school library, hunched over books, rereading sentences that grew blurry as he fought off sleep. He was determined to succeed in this second attempt at a career.

Moments of leisure and visits to family were rare. Yet somehow there were women, women met in class or by chance. There were dates -- lunch, a free lecture or concert, an occasional movie. In a few instances friendship blossomed into intimacy, and when Kramer brought a woman up the stairs to his room, it would be past the curious eyes of other residents in the house, people living alone like himself.

They peered from behind doors that were opened only a crack, or paused to look while standing in the hall. Kramer expected their curiosity to subside with familiarity and time, but it only increased. Was his bed noisy, he wondered? Then there was the music student, a woman from Virginia who was studying voice; after a few moments of lovemaking her sounds would begin, soft sighs at first, rising and growing progressively louder as if she were practicing scales, culminating finally in a piercing scream.

Kramer had never heard anything like it before and feared his neighbors would call the police; despite the lateness of the hour, every door was ajar when he left to take the woman home.

The women came and went during his student years -- fleeting encounters squeezed in between papers and exams. Like fireworks, these incandescent moments quickly sputtered away. It was only three years later, when he obtained his first academic job, that a more extended involvement developed.

The job offer had come suddenly, unexpectedly, at the end of July. His dissertation advisor had heard of a vacancy for the fall semester.

"Dan, they're looking for an instructor. It's a last minute thing -- a professor had a serious heart attack and he'll be out for at least a semester. There's no time for a search--they need someone right away. It's only a temporary appointment. Are you interested?"

"Very interested, where is it?"

"Pennsylvania. Nueland College. A small school, not far from Philadelphia. That's where you're from, isn't it?"

"Yes."

"You ought to contact them right away. Call the chairman of the psych department -- Tom Bordman."

If he got the job, it would mean leaving the furnished room that had been home for three years. No more shared bathroom, wailing sirens, pneumatic drills, hot city pavements in the summer; no more dodging beggars and derelicts. It would be an end to hyper vigilance -- that extra sense acquired by the big city dweller to warn against the assailant who could materialize out of nowhere. He'd give up music, museums, theatre, but who had money for culture? The affluent and the tourists, not struggling residents like himself. On the day of his interview he took the train to 30th Street Station in Philadelphia where he changed to the Paoli Local, then a bus to Nueland. Riding through the rolling countryside of Chester County for the first time, he saw picture postcard hamlets, horse country, Wyeth farms with red barns and post-and-rail fences. This was where he wanted to be.

The campus was a short distance from the center of town. Walking along Main Street, Kramer passed a small shopping center, then a block or two of older brick fronted row homes that now housed boutiques and offices of lawyers and physicians. The July afternoon was sunny and hot; he carried his jacket over his arm. He had been tempted to wear an open-collared short-sleeved shirt; he knew college dress was casual.

But this was a special occasion, one in which an impression would be made; he decided to be safe and wear a jacket and tie.

Turning off Main on to Chestnut, he came upon a stretch of Georgian homes that had been restored. Old trees gave the street a lush softness. He was drawn to the atmosphere of the town, so unlike the concrete grittiness of Manhattan, yet more animated and engaging than the sleepy streets he had seen in South Carolina on his High Holiday experience as a student rabbi. He was soon on the edge of the campus, with its outlying offices in former homes, each identified by a black-lettered sign posted on the lawn: Admissions, Student Affairs, Alumni Relations, and Graduate Studies. He reached one of the main buildings and entered a cool Gothic archway; the enclosed grassy quadrangle opened before him like a magic garden. A student directed him to the department of psychology.

At a desk near the door, a sweet mannered older woman with a welcoming smile seemed to be expecting him. She directed Kramer to the chairman's office, where a heavy set man in a short sleeved, open-collared shirt rose and extended his hand. "Hi. I'm Tom Bordman."

Kramer sat in a chair alongside the cluttered desk. Bordman stepped to the door and closed it, muffling the sounds and student voices coming from the secretary's office.

"How was your trip?"

"Fine."

Bordman leaned back in his chair and spoke of Kramer's thesis chairman; they had gone to graduate school together. He then asked about Kramer's research interests and dissertation.

"I'm doing a follow-up study of Stonequist's work--the Marginal Man."

"Social psych."

"Yes."

Bordman nodded and quickly turned to the immediate situation. "This is the story. We need a temporary instructor for the fall semester -- that's in less than two months. One of our faculty recently went on sick leave. I've had to juggle courses and schedules; there are four intro sections that need to be covered. Could you take them?"

Kramer hesitated, not wishing to appear too eager.

"I know four intros aren't very exciting--I guess you'd rather teach social psych or personality. But that's the situation. It'll get your foot in the door, if you want to teach."

"I'm interested," Kramer said. He got the job.

He did well enough to be offered a contract for the following year, and then moved into a tenure-track assistant professorship that developed when the sick professor retired.

While his classes were large, the teaching load of four sections of introductory psychology required only one preparation, giving him enough time to speed up work on his doctoral dissertation. But when that task was finally completed, rather than feeling the joy of achievement that he had anticipated, Kramer found himself caught in an undertow of depression.

Sitting alone in his one bedroom apartment night after night, listening to his records or staring blankly at the moving images on his small television set, he realized that with a goal achieved, he was now confronted with loneliness. He himself was an example of the marginal man he'd studied; a newcomer on the edge of academia, one of the few Jews in a provincial college that had just begun accepting Jewish faculty. True, Tom Bordman had invited him once to his home for dinner, and there had been a couple of departmental parties, but he was an alien among the others--professors from the South, the West. Beer drinkers exuding a forced cheeriness who listened to raucous music he could not abide.

It was at one of these parties, as he sat alone, fighting a desire to get up and leave, that a woman, older than students, but younger than faculty, approached him.

"You look like you need someone to take care of you," she said. "Can I get you something? A drink?"

She was pleasant enough, a smallish woman with long black hair, and he felt no impulse to resist her.

"Is there any wine?" he asked.

She left, returning soon with two plastic cups, one with white wine for him. He glanced at her cup and she explained, "I prefer diet Coke."

As he sipped his wine she watched him with a faintly amused smile that made him uncomfortable.

"You don't recognize me," she said. "I'm in your four o'clock class. Claire Miller."

"Of course! I'm so sorry!"

"That's okay," she said. "It's a big class."

Before he could say more she had slipped away, blending into the crowd.

He remembered her now. She was older than most of his students. She sat up front, directly facing him, yet at the beginning of the semester he didn't really notice her.

She never spoke or raised her hand; her appearance and dress were nondescript. Like a small animal with protective coloring, she faded into the human landscape in the room.

It was her intensity that finally made him aware of her. He soon realized that she was hanging on to his every word, and that her large brown eyes were fixed upon him as he moved about the room. He guessed that her behavior was an expression of the seriousness he often saw in the older returning student whose education had been interrupted by the demands of career or family.

Her black hair hung loosely about her face when she looked down to take notes. As she raised her head he saw that the skin under her eyes looked faintly smudged, perhaps making her appear older and less attractive, yet her glance had a smoldering quality that drew him to her. At the conclusion of each of his lectures, during the rustle of books and papers, she took longer than the others to leave and was still collecting her things as he headed for the door. Walking down the hall he sensed that she was behind him. He turned but she looked away.

Kramer was surprised when she received a low grade on her first exam. He didn't give her much further thought until he met her at the party. The following week he read a paper she had submitted.

It was a class assignment, an analysis of the personality of an acquaintance, drawing upon personality theory. His students dropped off their papers on his desk as they filed out of the room. At home that night, Kramer began reading the submitted papers; most described a relative or a friend, one or two were self-portraits. The opening of Claire Miller's paper caught his attention.

"I decided to change my life the morning I awoke in a motel room and didn't know how I got there. A man, a stranger, was sitting on the edge of the bed, and an empty bottle of Jack Daniel's was on the night table. I realized that if I kept it up, I would destroy myself."

The paper went on to describe Claire's uneducated working class family, her own barren existence, and the sudden hunger for knowledge and culture which developed after her decision to change her life. On the day of that decision, she registered for her first course at the college. Since then, she had been taking one course a semester towards a degree. She worked in a bank.

In her self-analysis, Claire drew upon both Freud and Adler. Freud, to shed light on her yearning for a good father; Adler, for her belief that she could change her life. While not outstanding, the paper was strong and honest and Kramer could see that much effort had gone into the writing. It was a long paper, and the personal revelations required courage.

In the next exam Claire received a failing grade. Kramer carefully went over the scoring, hoping to find an error; there was none. The grades were posted and when the class met, Kramer could see that Claire was upset; she lingered at the end of the hour, waiting for the others to leave.

"I'd like to make an appointment," she said.

She arrived on a chilly October afternoon; with a shy smile she took the seat beside his desk, still wearing her hooded jacket. Her face, framed in white synthetic fleece, was flushed by the cold. She radiated the innocence a child coming in from the snow; to Kramer she seemed so unlike the person she had described in her paper.

"You can take your coat off."

"Oh." She rose and struggled out of the coat and dropped it on a chair. When she seemed settled, Kramer said, "I guess you've come because of your exam."

She nodded.

"Let's go over it."

He pulled the exam from his file and reviewed each question and her reply. She immediately grasped the correct answers as he explained them to her.

"Why didn't I see that?" she murmured. "I'm so stupid."

"No, no," Kramer insisted. "You just didn't absorb the material."

"But I went over it three times -- the readings, my notes."

He asked her about her other courses. She had only taken a few, mostly business and accounting.

He suggested how she could improve her study skills -- identifying main ideas, putting them in writing.

She was absent at the next meeting of his class and throughout his lecture he was conscious of her empty chair. A day later he received a note from the registrar's office stating that she had withdrawn from his course.

Withdrawals occurred from time to time for a variety of reasons -- illness, perhaps an overloaded schedule. Kramer waited for the withdrawal to fade from his attention, but found himself preoccupied with it. Had he unwittingly offended the girl? Did something happen to her? He was tempted to find out by calling, but realized this would be inappropriate -- he certainly hadn't done so before. Students had the right to drop courses without being subjected to telephone interrogations by their professors.

But the question continued to nag at him; he finally obtained her phone number from the registrar's office. He called her that evening; her hello sounded stronger and more assertive than he had anticipated.

"This is Professor Kramer," he said.

"Oh."

"Are you all right?"

"Yes -- I'm all right."

He suddenly felt foolish and defensive. "I'm calling because I see that you've dropped my course. I thought something might have happened."

"No. It's just -- I wasn't making it."

"Maybe you gave up too easily."

"I didn't want to flunk."

"I see." He paused, and then said quickly, "I'd like you to try again. I think you can do it. I'll help you."

"Oh, you're very kind. But I really tried -- maybe I just have to accept the fact that I'm not cut out for college..."

"No." He was pushing the issue and couldn't understand why. "I'd like you to come in--tomorrow--so we might talk about this."

She finally agreed; she would come directly from work--he would be there, an hour earlier than the customary arrival time for his evening class.

They spent the hour going over work she had missed. Her face grew brighter as she realized she was mastering the material. Then he offered to see her every week at the same time.

"Oh no, that's so sweet of you," she said. "But I couldn't do that."

"Why not?"

"What a terrible imposition! I could never --"

"Please. I want to do it."

She said nothing. The skin under her eyes seemed a shade darker; she was scrutinizing him and he wondered if she thought him strange. What if she asked him the reason for his insistence? He couldn't tell her why; he didn't know.

"Let's give it a try," he said, finally ending the silence.

She agreed.

Between their meetings he thought about her a good deal of the time, and discovered, to his surprise, that his depression had lifted. His preoccupation grew stronger and waiting to see her became increasingly difficult for him. He thought of driving by Claire's house to catch a glimpse of her. But then she would see him and be aware of his craziness; the exposure would be humiliating.

She passed the next exam, and in fact obtained a good grade. When Kramer arrived at his office for their meeting, Claire was already there, waiting at the door; as soon as they were inside she handed him a small package.

"For you," she said, smiling.

He removed the red ribbon and gift wrapping; it was a silver pen set, engraved with his name.

"I'm so grateful," she said. "You have no idea how much you've helped me."

Too flustered to speak, he put the gift on his desk, then finally murmured, "You really shouldn't --"

This time she didn't remove her coat.

"I feel I can manage alone now," she said. "I just wanted to stop by and thank you."

He felt he must tell her not to go, but could say nothing. She reached out and hugged him; he yearned to respond, but the very intensity of his desire paralyzed him.

Then she was gone.

She continued to do well. When he saw her in class he nodded and she smiled but they didn't speak.

Much to his relief, he found his preoccupation with Claire subsiding. Perhaps his interest in her had been only academic after all--a desire to help a student who had potential, but was in danger of wasting it. He recalled her paper and its description of the wild person she had once been. It was best that he had avoided crossing the line between classroom and intimacy. There were too many risks: Claire's unpredictability, the whispered scandal that could trail colleagues involved with students, and the possibly damaging impact on his hopes for tenure.

Then one day, when the semester had ended, he found her standing in front of his office door.

"What a surprise!" he said.

He invited her in; she stood in the middle of the room, looking at him.

"I miss you," she said.

He struggled with a response. An embrace? He fought off the impulse. A kind, understanding word? It would be patronizing. A casual flip comment? He could not trivialize her feelings.

She watched his silent paralysis for what seemed endless moments, then spun around and hurried out of the room.

Chapter 12

He couldn't completely forget her. From time to time, startled, he thought he saw her on campus, but it always turned out to be someone else. He tried to shake off the persistent residue of his preoccupation--her image, the black hair, and the shadowy, feverish eyes. When efforts to reason with himself failed, Kramer decided on a change of tactic; rather than think less about her, he'd think more, willfully producing thoughts that were negative.

Building a fantasy superstructure on what he knew from her paper, he saw her as a promiscuous alcoholic, a woman whose wild hedonism was precariously controlled. The excessive restraint she displayed was bound to collapse at some point; the consequences would be disastrous. This was a woman who could destroy others as well as herself.

The fantasy didn't work as intended. Instead of being repelled, the wildness he imagined drew Kramer closer. Over and over he reviewed their last encounter, regretting the lost opportunity, the idiocy of his response. She was angry when she left; she had seen his paralysis as a humiliating rejection.

He did see her again. It was over a year later, in September, at registration. He was sitting at the department table in the gym. The doors opened and a mass of waiting students descended upon tables lined up along the bare walls.

Each table, attended by two faculty members, was identified by a large black-lettered placard: Philosophy, Secondary Ed, Mathematics, Psychology, and English. Kramer was talking to a freshman standing in front of his table when he suddenly spotted Claire moving about in the center of the crowd, appearing lost. She must have noticed him too -- she headed quickly for the Mathematics table on the other side of the gym.

Kramer had to pull his attention back to the student facing him. "Social Psychology is closed," he said. "You could go to class on the first day and see if anyone dropped the course. Or try next semester -- it'll be scheduled again."

He continued giving his half-attention to the students in his line, all the time thinking of her, trying to follow her path from table to table. She would walk by his table eventually to complete her registration; or she might leave and return the next day when he wouldn't be there. Then he saw her heading for the exit.

Muttering "Just a minute" to the next student in line, Kramer rose and hurried across the polished gym floor, pushing his way through the crowd, finally reaching her in the outside hall. He put his hand on her shoulder and she turned to face him.

"Hello," he said.

She pulled away and hurried to the building exit, but he followed her.

"Wait!"

His heart was racing now and he felt foolish; he was an idiot, a teen-ager like the students who were turning to look at him. She stopped on the path near some hedges and he caught up with her.

"Look," he said. "I was hoping I'd see you again. I'd like to talk to you. Can we have coffee together?"

She shook her head. "I have to go."

"Well -- can't we set up a time?"

"I'd rather not." She turned and he pulled her back.

"Please. I really want to see you."

Hesitant, she seemed to be examining his face. Then she pushed back her hair in a quick gesture and said, unsmiling, "I have Thursday afternoon off."

He was elated. "Fine, let's have lunch together on Thursday."

They met in a fast-food restaurant on the Pike, a truck stop not frequented by students or faculty. Her features were the same--the lusterless black hair, the dark searching eyes--yet she seemed different. It was not just the slight change produced by the passage of time. A softness of expression was missing. He hadn't been aware of the softness a year earlier, but now for the first time he realized it had been a part of her.

"How have you been?"

She hesitated, and then said, "Okay, I guess."

She glanced at him, waiting. She didn't ask, but it was clear that she wanted him to explain. Why were they meeting? What did he want of her? His glasses were misting; he reached into his back pocket for his handkerchief and wiped them. She wasn't making it easy for him, so he decided to be direct.

"I was surprised to see you on campus again. It's been over a year." She looked down at her salad, her face partially obscured by her long hair. He wanted to reach out, brush her hair back, and stroke her cheek.

"I've missed you," he said. "Do you believe me?"

She remained silent. He asked, "What happened to you?"

"I dropped out."

"Oh."

"Just school." She looked up. "I kept working, but I had to get away from school. I didn't think I'd ever return."

"Why?"

"I was in love with you."

He watched her in stunned silence.

She gave a slight smile. "It's over. That's why I'm back."

She had recovered and was free of him. It was as though she had vanquished an illness, one for which he had been somehow responsible.

"And now that I'm here with you," she said, "I can see for myself that it's really over."

"Sort of a test."

She smiled. "Yes."

She agreed to see him again. He wished that somehow her old feeling for him could be resurrected, but when they met a week later it seemed that Claire was intent on pushing him away. She told him that the year had been painful, that she had seen many men in her effort cure herself of her obsession with him. She spoke freely of a reckless life, of her fear of becoming an alcoholic like her father. Her

58

disclosures made him want her more. Kramer warned himself that it would be a bad relationship. He had become the needy one, the pursuer. She had grown stronger. If the relationship continued and deepened, there would be complications; his parents would be pained by his involvement with a non-Jewish woman.

But these concerns were easily overwhelmed by his feelings. Claire continued to see him, and her tone remained detached, at times amused. Even when they began making love, he felt she was being agreeable, condescending, not really there. The first time he looked at her body she laughed, "Now you see that I'm really a dumb blonde."

He wanted to ask, "Why do you see me? You show no feeling--you seem to be playing with me." But he feared the question would displease her and kept it to himself.

His small one bedroom apartment was on Chestnut Street, three blocks from the campus. They met there on Thursday afternoons; he changed his office hours to free up the time. They never spoke of it, but he didn't want the relationship to be visible to the campus community. A love affair between a professor and a student --why be the object of campus gossip and scrutiny? And she was a private person who wanted to maintain her anonimity. The prospect of whispers and knowing glances--"she's Kramer's girlfriend"--repelled her.

On Thursday afternoons he stood near the door of his apartment waiting for the sound of her steps, his heart beating more rapidly and his body growing aroused as the time for her arrival drew closer. Then came the flash of elation when he heard the rustle of her presence on the other side of the door, and then the soft knock.

When with Claire he thought only of the moment: holding her, making love in his narrow bed, never being fully sated. At times, when alone, he thought of their future together. Would he, the son of a rabbi, a former observant Jew and rabbinical student--would he take the next step in abandoning his past and intermarry?

At times he awoke at night, asking why he had gotten into such a situation. The sensible thing would be to get out of it at once, spare his parents the pain, and spare himself the ordeal of telling them. He regularly rehearsed the dreaded scene, the revelation that he was "seeing someone." It would be during one of his increasingly less frequent visits--perhaps on Passover. He went every year to participate in his father's Seder--the last holdover from the past. He saw his attendance as an attachment to family rather than an expression of religious belief. And the holiday had a secular dimension to which he couldn't object--the celebration of freedom.

Sooner or later--perhaps during a Seder meal after they chanted the story of the Exodus and the soup had been served, the subject would come up. Questions about his future--career, marriage--would emerge, more likely brought forth by his mother with a gentle smile. This time he would announce, "I'm seeing someone." Exclamations of pleased surprise by both of his parents would follow, then questions in a playful tone, and finally it would all come out: she was a former student, working class family, uncultured, not Jewish. Father a sullen man, an alcoholic, perhaps recovering. Mother gushingly sentimental, insincere, shallow and an auto mechanic brother.

Stunned silence. Then his father's questions. Was it serious? Would she convert? He wouldn't tell them how much he wanted her that marriage was his hope, not hers; that conversion had come up once, and when she dismissed it with a quick laugh he vowed not to mention it again.

They might ask, Why? What did he see in her? He could tell them he had asked himself the identical question, many times. It was a question he couldn't answer. For it wasn't a matter of logic or reason. If it were, he could end it. The mental rehearsals continued, but the actual event never took place. His father died before Passover.

"They took him to the hospital," she said. "They called. He's gone." Sobbing, she fell into her son's arms. He led her away from the door into the living room, and then helped her to the sofa. He sat with her in silence, flooded with memories of his father: the walks to the synagogue before dawn; his father holding the silver wine goblet in his hand as he stood chanting the Kiddush before the Sabbath table; the sermons from the podium in the old synagogue before the hushed congregation; summers at the shore. Then he suddenly realized, looking at his mother as she stared into space, that it was he who would have to make all the arrangements.

He called the college. "My father died," he heard himself say. "I'll be out-- for a week." Then, the calls to the funeral parlor, relatives, and an old colleague of his father with the request that he officiate at the funeral. Then, before phoning the newspapers, a quick mental review of the details that would sum up his father's life.

He didn't mention Claire to his mother, and she was too preoccupied with her loss to ask him difficult questions.

Chapter 13

Claire arrived every Thursday afternoon and Kramer's fear that he would lose her gradually faded. As they lay in bed she began to speak more freely, and one afternoon she surprised him with her directness.

"This is getting to be boring," she said. "All we do is go to bed."

"Is that boring?"

"I want more."

"More of what?"

"You're educated," she said. "You're a professor. You know a lot--about books, plays and art, as well as psychology.

That's what I want, to know more about all these things. I feel so ignorant. I want to become a cultured person. All we do is fuck. You don't even talk to me."

He was stunned by the accusation. Resting on her elbow, she was looking down at him as she spoke. He wanted to calm her, to ease her anger; he reached up and pushed back her hair, stroked her face, her arm, then her breast. She pulled away.

"That's what I mean. You're not talking, you're grabbing.

Sex is fine, but I can get that anywhere. I want you to talk."

"About what?"

"Anything. Psychology--you're a psychology professor and you never talk to me about deep things, literature, art, history. I want to learn from you. Why do you think I went back to school? I feel so uneducated, so stupid. I don't want to end up like my family--my mother."

His surprise at her outburst quickly shifted to anxiety. Had he been condescending? Was she tired of him?

"I'll be happy to talk to you," he said.

"Okay. But not just about sex or where to eat. I have to make up for lost time. I admire educated, cultured people.

That's what attracted me to you in the first place. You don't think it was because you're sexy, do you?"

He laughed, but then saw that she was serious.

"I didn't realize how ignorant it was, until a few years ago. Until I went through that crisis I wrote about in my paper."

"I don't think you're ignorant at all. You're a bright woman."

"Yeah. Street smarts. But as far as culture is concerned, I'm ignorant."

"Of course I'll talk to you," he said, now sitting up beside her. "But you don't expect me to give you a lecture every Thursday. Or do you?"

"I just want you to stop talking to me like I was in the fifth grade. I want you to use words I don't know, and explain them. I want you to tell me about your ideas, your background--stuff that I can learn from you."

"I will, I promise, and I'm sorry if I treated you badly. It wasn't intentional."

"I know, it was unconscious," she said, still not smiling.

"And I don't want us just to meet and screw. We should do things, like go to museums and concerts, classical music.

I've never seen a live opera. Why can't we go to Philadelphia or New York to see an opera? Or a play?" "Of course we can. But then we'll be seen in public. You didn't want that."

"I know, but I feel differently now. Are we gonna hide out forever? So what if people gossip--would it bother you?"

He reached out and hugged her. "I don't care what people think."

They kissed and he wanted her, but she pushed him away.

"Things will be different," he said. "I promise."

From that day on he always had classical music playing when she visited. He suggested books, and as she read them they would discuss the content and her impressions, then his. He lent her volumes from his library--Steinbeck, Maugham, Hemingway. She preferred short stories and novels to non-fiction. He read the papers she wrote for her classes and reviewed them with her. She developed an immediate liking for Tchaikovsky and Schubert. He took her to a

Philadelphia Orchestra concert; she loved the Grieg Piano Concerto but was restless during Prokofiev's Fifth Symphony.

"It was awful," she told him as they were driving home. "I don't see how anyone could like it. It's just a lot of noise."

"That's the way music often sounds the first time."

"Did you like it?"

"Yes. You ought to listen to some of Prokofiev's other works-- the music for Romeo and Juliet. If you see the ballet with the music- -I saw it a couple of times on television--you might get to like Prokofiev. Or see the movie Alexander Nevsky. He composed the music."

She wrote the titles on a scrap of paper. When Kramer saw her a week later, she had bought recordings of both Romeo and Juliet and Alexander Nevsky. She loved Romeo and Juliet and had played it countless times. One Thursday she arrived at his door with a folder clutched in her hand. He reached out to embrace her and she moved away.

"I brought along a paper," she said, handing him the folder. "I need your help with it."

It was clear that the paper would be the first order of business for the afternoon. "It's only a rough draft," she said, walking to his small kitchen and sitting at the table "For my English class. We're studying about Kafka- the writer. We have to do a paper on the meaning of one of his stories--Meta." She paused. "I don't know how to pronounce it."

"Metamorphosis," he said, going over the word several times with her until she could repeat it with ease. Then she asked, "What does it mean?"

"Change."

"'Change?' Like in nickels and dimes?"

He couldn't suppress a laugh and quickly apologized, but it was too late; her face flushed with anger, she rose and moved toward the door. He rushed to her and grasped her arm.

"Please don't go. I'm really very sorry."

"You were laughing at me!"

"I couldn't help myself. Please forgive me. I really want to help you. I was an idiot ... it won't happen again."

Looking uncertain, she finally relented and stepped back to the kitchen table.

"Well? Are you going to tell me what the word means?"

He proceeded with an elaborate explanation, giving a variety of examples; caterpillar and moth, bud and flower—

"Oh, I see," she interrupted. "He's a person who changes into a cockroach. That's the metamorphosis."

"Yes, exactly."

"Okay. Now we can go over the paper. The professor sometimes asks students to read their papers to the class. I'll go over it--I'll read it to you, sentence by sentence, and you stop me any time with changes or corrections I should make. Okay?"

"Fine, go ahead."

She began reading slowly, and almost at once he saw himself with Annamarie, seated at a corner of the library table, listening to her hesitant reading of Hebrew prayers in her Siddur. The memory, sudden and powerful, misted his eyes. He wondered what had happened to Annamarie, and then he thought of Himmelshine as well, again seeing them emerging together from a cab that night. Was that to be his fate? Loving women, only to be abandoned by them?

"Well? Are you listening?"

"Of course," he said quickly. "My mind wandered there for a minute. Just repeat the last two sentences."

She paused, looking at him with annoyance, and then resumed her reading. He made running corrections and suggestions, pausing as she bent over her paper, making notes. When she finished, he rose, saying, "Not bad."

She quickly put her things together and hurried to the door. Without looking back, she said, "We're late ... I gotta go."

He was able to get tickets for a Saturday matinee performance of Aida at the Metropolitan. They took the train to New York in the morning; it was hard for him to believe that she had never been to Manhattan. As they rode by cab to Lincoln Center, the driver navigating through wild currents of heavy traffic, Claire was staring incredulously out of the window at the passing scene. While she was in awe over the electric excitement of the city, he saw the grime and decay.

They were pressed forward by the crowd in the lobby and were soon settled in their seats. Claire stared about at the glamorous vastness of the hall, its balconies and chandelier, then opened her program, found the synopsis of the opera and became engrossed in it. Her dread, she had told Kramer, was that she would fail to comprehend what was happening on the stage, doomed to sit for hours trapped in ignorance.

When the opera and curtain calls finally came to an end, she was still applauding after others in their row had left.

"You liked it?" Kramer asked.

"It was wonderful."

Kramer too had enjoyed the performance, but focused much of his attention on Claire, her face smiling and radiant in the semi-darkness. And the opera brought to mind thoughts that he didn't share with her: ancient Egypt made him think of The Exodus and Passover; the bound Ethiopian captives on the stage, hands extended in supplication, reminded him of the enslaved Children of Israel.

Chapter 14

Claire displayed a continuing hunger to learn, and her growing sophistication surprised him. Her reading increased, mostly classic novels like those he had lent her, and she regularly sought his guidance, saving unfamiliar words and concepts for him to explain.

She invited him to dinner. "I want you to meet my family," she said.

When he hesitated, she asked, "What's the matter? Don't you want to come?"

"I'm just surprised."

"Why?"

"The way you've described your family--you don't seem to like them very much. I'm surprised you'd want us to meet."

"Look, I'm not proud of them. But still, they're my family. I think it's time to introduce you."

He was feeling uneasy, knowing that if he met her family she would expect to meet his mother. And how could he tell his mother about Claire?

"Don't you think it's time?" Claire asked. "We've been seeing each other for almost two years. Everybody at the college knows about us – that doesn't seem to bother you. Shouldn't you meet my family?"

He nodded his agreement.

"And I'll meet your mother--if she wants to see me."

He was silent.

"Does she want to see me?"

He tensed, but knew he had to be honest.

"I haven't told her about you yet."

Her eyes widened. "You haven't?"

"You know that my mother is quite old --"

"Are you ashamed of me?"

"Of course not! I love you."

"Well--why haven't you told your mother?"

"She's a religious woman. She hasn't gotten over the death of my father. I don't want to upset her."

"You mean because I'm not a Jew?"

He hesitated, and then said, "Yes."

Claire was silent. It was Saturday night and they were having dinner at L'Aiglon, the only French restaurant in town.

Kramer listened to the mournful voice of Edith Piaf coming from the speaker behind the small bar in a corner of the poster-lined room. Claire had stopped eating; she was staring down at the candle flame inside the glass lamp on their table. Finally she looked up at him.

"I thought you were joking that day when you talked about my converting."

He shook his head. "It would make life much easier for us." He watched her closely, hoping that somehow she would agree.

"Not easier for us," she said. "Easier for you. I still feel the same way about it. Not that I have anything against Jews or Judaism. I really don't care much for any religion. I just want to be what I am."

He lowered his head, thinking of his mother's pain.

Finally he said, "I understand."

She paused, and then asked, "Is this going to be a problem? I mean, is it going to get between us?"

"I hope not. It shouldn't. We'll find a way."

"Will you tell your mother?"

He saw his mother's response: silent disbelief as she sat in the corner of the old sofa in the living room, then her continued silence as she looked away from him. Anger? She rarely displayed open anger; instead, she would bow her head in resignation, which would be more difficult for him to bear.

Claire said, "I guess you don't want to tell her. Do you plan to keep it a secret? Wait until she's gone? Is that it?"

"Please, Claire..." He reached out and took her hand. "I'll tell her. It won't be easy or pleasant. But it's reality. I want us to have a life together."

Chapter 15

Her brother Mike met them at the door; stout, with a genial smile, he extended his hand.

"Pleased to meet you," he said. "Come on in."

They entered a tiny vestibule, and then stepped into a dark living room with a stale smell. Oversized brown upholstered furniture with doilies everywhere first caught Kramer's eye, then religious pictures on the walls, and then he saw Claire's father sitting in a corner, watching a baseball game on television. A balding unsmiling man with a ruddy face, he nodded to Kramer, then turned his attention back to the game.

Claire's mother stepped out of the kitchen, wiping her hands on her apron before extending it in greeting.

"Hello!" she said, with loud enthusiasm, smiling broadly.

She was a short, gray-haired woman, and Kramer was taken by her warmth, until he realized the smile was constant, regardless of what was being said--part of a persona of unending cheeriness. "We've heard so much about you from Claire--it's nice to meet you."

Kramer thanked her, and then Mike asked, "How about a beer?"

Kramer said okay, and Mike added, "We're watching the game. Why don't you have a seat?"

Kramer took the corner of the sofa pointed out by Mike, and as he settled back, Claire's father shot a glance at him, and then returned to the game. Claire was in the kitchen with her mother, and as Mike handed him a cold beer can, Kramer wished she would join him and ease the feeling of entrapped alienation that gripped him.

From time to time Mike made comments about the game, and his father, mostly silent, would grunt a response. The game moved ahead slowly, and Kramer was now conscious of the discomfort of his seat; he had sunk deeply into the sofa and could feel its broken springs. Finally Claire emerged from the kitchen and sat at his side, whispering, "Dinner will be ready soon."

As a result of coincidence or practiced timing by Claire's mother, dinner was announced just as the game ended. At the table, Kramer discovered that Mr. Miller's silence was not a consequence of being engrossed in the game, but a fixed personality trait--Claire's father rarely spoke. His wife made up for the silence, producing a stream of chatter--about the weather, her neighbors, the condition of the town, the importance of education.

"You're a professor at the college, Claire says. Is that right?"

"Yes."

"What kind of a professor are you?"

"He teaches Psychology."

"Oh, now isn't that interesting!" Her mother went on to explain how she and her husband had to leave school when young in order to go to work, and that Claire was the first member of the family to attend college. "My family didn't put much stock in schooling. We all had to work, my brothers and sisters. We were a big family -- ten children."

Kramer nodded, at first waiting for a pause to offer an understanding comment or two, but then finding that pauses were not taking place. Claire's mother went on and on with an extended monologue, not expecting any response; she just wanted to express herself, to be listened to, and Kramer gave up waiting for a break in the verbal traffic. Nodding agreement from time to time, he concentrated on his soup. Interruptions occurred when Mrs. Miller went into the kitchen to bring out another dish--salad, a lamb stew— but at these times Claire joined her to assist, and Kramer, facing the prospect of silence, asked Mike about his work and learned that he was a mechanic in a local Ford agency.

"I noticed three cars in the driveway," Kramer said. "Do you also work at home?"

Mike smiled. "Those are old Pontiacs. There are four more in the back yard. I work for Ford, but my hobby is old Pontiacs. I love them. I fix them up and sell them. I hate giving them up--they're great old cars."

"He's a real Pontiac nut," Mr. Miller said, startling Kramer, who had gotten to accept the man's silence.

"Dad thinks I clutter the place up," Mike said. Kramer searched for some comment to encourage further talk by Mr. Miller when Claire and her mother emerged from the kitchen with lemon meringue pie and coffee. The mother's monologue resumed at once and continued until the dinner ended. As the dishes were being cleared, Mr. Miller rose from the table and went to the living room, back to his chair facing the television set. Mike followed his father, as though this was the familiar and natural thing to do, and Kramer too returned to his spot in the corner of the sofa, wondering when the evening would end.

Chapter 16

It was September and only a few weeks until Yom Kippur; he decided to wait until after the holiday before telling his mother. The fading of summer always aroused a vague sense of foreboding that he associated with the coming of the High Holidays. The new academic year, faculty meetings, returning students milling in the halls--all the college bustle failed to mask the persistent sensation of dread. Kramer tried to attribute the feeling to the death of summer, with its early dusk and windy chill. But such attribution, he realized, could only be partially valid. Despite his intellectual rejection of the past, his mood was still colored by the approaching Days of Awe.

He didn't teach on Rosh Hashanah and Yom Kippur out of deference to the few students and faculty who observed the holiday. While he might venture out in the afternoon on Rosh Hashanah when people would not expect him to be in synagogue, he spent the whole day of Yom Kippur closed up in his apartment. Reading, ruminating, wandering aimlessly from room to room, he waited for the long day to end.

Yom Kippur was one of the two most difficult days of the year for Kramer; the other was Christmas. At opposite ideological and emotional extremes, the two holidays produced an identical impact upon him, that of alienation. On Yom Kippur he could not help but think of Jews throughout the world gathered in crowded synagogues, families together in prayer, and he, the voluntary exile, no longer among them. On Christmas too he was the outsider, watching the passing parade, observing the puzzling joyousness of someone else's party.

The somber mood of the High Holidays was accompanied by memories: the aura of reverence surrounding the candle-lit dining room table; the hush that descended upon the packed synagogue when his father, in his penitential white gown, would begin his sermon; the primeval echoes of Kol Nidre.

After Yom Kippur, as after Christmas, his life would regularly resume, like a movie halted in mid-frame suddenly returning to motion. The alienation was gone; he was relieved to find himself once again among the others.

When he drove to Philadelphia to tell his mother about Claire, the neighborhood still retained the character he recalled from the past: leafy streets, modest twin homes with adjoining open porches, small front lawns and backyard gardens. During his childhood the white middle-class and lower middle-class population gave no hint of the eventual multicolored racial mix. Broad Street, the spine of the neighborhood, still had store signs in English, not Korean or Vietnamese; the two or three synagogues had not yet evolved into union halls, black churches, and then exotic oriental temples.

Despite urging since the death of his father, Kramer's mother declined to move into a retirement residence. The stairs in the old house grew harder for her to climb, and while the cleaning woman she had for years still came once a week, keeping up the house was increasingly difficult. Maintenance was a growing problem, although on his periodic visits Kramer would make the small repairs his mother had accumulated for him.

The drive to Philadelphia eventually brought him to the Jewish enclave of his childhood, past the delicatessen, the synagogue, the Jewish bakery, the Kosher butcher shop. It was along this street that he had walked with his father on dark, quiet, clean-smelling mornings to the daily service. During his adolescent years the minyan, the quorum of ten worshipers, was already being maintained with some difficulty.

At times eight or nine men would be sitting about in the small basement chapel, waiting, and then, with the arrival of the rabbi and his son, the minyan was attained; men of varying ages and walks of life became a group: wearing phylacteries and prayer shawls, they chanted together as the cantor led them in prayer. Kramer remembered the good feeling of the early morning service, a communion of men radiating warmth and friendliness. The familiar, unchanging ritual served as a spiritual and emotional grounding for the remainder of the day.

He parked near the house and his mother came to the door as soon as he rang the bell. She must have been waiting, watching for his arrival through the front window. "Danny!" she called out, as though his visit were a surprise. She asked the familiar questions--about his trip, his health, his work--and then announced, "You must be hungry," and insisted that he eat. Favorite lunch dishes of his childhood--beet borscht with a dollop of sour cream, a salad with smoked white fish--were ready to be served.

He was no longer a professor but a little boy, seated at the familiar kitchen table, resuming contact with the smells and sights of the past. But the old furniture, bric-a-brac, pictures on the walls and family photos--all that would usually envelop him in a cozy, secure feeling of renewal--now produced uneasiness as he contemplated the news he would soon convey.

After inquiring about her health and listening to gossip about family and old members of his father's congregation,

"I have some news for you, Mom."

She turned to him suddenly, and he realized his tone had alerted her to a significant, perhaps ominous, development.

"I'm getting married."

The strain on her face was swept away by a wide smile.

"That's wonderful!" She rose with alacrity, hurried to him and gave him a kiss. "Mazel Tov!" Still smiling, she said, "If only your father were alive to hear this! You've been keeping a secret from me! How long have you known her?"

"Two years. She's a former student of mine."

"Ah hah! She must be much younger than you."

"She is. Her name is Claire."

"Claire?"

"Yes. Claire Miller."

"I'd love to meet her."

"Of course."

"She's Jewish?"

He tensed and took a deep breath. "No. She's a good person, but she's not Jewish."

His mother's face clouded and the network of wrinkles in her forehead and cheeks deepened, as if her aging had accelerated right before him. She remained silent, and then released a deep sigh. After a long pause, she said, "I'm sure she's a lovely person."

His eyes misted. "I know this upsets you, Mom --"

"Of course it upsets me! Is she converting?"

"No. Claire doesn't practice any religion and is too honest to convert."

His mother reached for her small embroidered handkerchief.

"It's so sad, so sad," she lamented. "It's the end--the end of the family. Our only son, thousands of years--so much suffering--we managed to survive--and now it's over, ending."

"Mother ..."

He wished for some words to ease her pain but nothing came to him. Helpless, he watched as she dabbed her eyes.

"We love each other," he said at last. "She's a fine woman. You'll see."

"I don't want to see."

He remained silent and she turned to him, a note of apology in her voice. "I just can't do it. I can't meet her. Not now, but maybe someday. "

She sighed again, a deeper, anguished sigh, as though it were not hers alone but that of many, reaching back in time.

"I'm only glad your father didn't live to see this."

Chapter 17

Claire had moved into Kramer's one bedroom apartment in an older red brick row house near campus. The three-story house, like several on the block, had been converted into apartment units, two on each floor.

"We don't have enough room here," Claire said. "Let's buy a house."

Kramer found the suggestion to be disturbing. Claire looked at him, puzzled.

"You seem upset" she said. "We're both working--we can afford an inexpensive house. This place is always a mess--clothes and books piled up everywhere. We only have two closets here--we need more room. We're getting married soon--why not buy a house?"

Kramer asked himself the same question, and then realized that home ownership would give their relationship solidity. Perhaps he saw their relationship as being loose, non-binding and reversible. He somehow felt that even after a wedding, the tie could be broken and freedom would still be an option. But the concreteness of jointly owning a house, with its physical reality, meant permanence.

But did he want the option of escape? Of course not, he told himself. He loved Claire; he didn't want their relationship to be just an affair, which she as well as he could end easily.

"Okay," he finally said to her. "Let's do it."

He asked colleagues, home owners who knew the community, to recommend a real estate agent, and the house hunting began. Kramer and Claire spent week-ends making the rounds of open houses near the college, as well as getting leads from their agent. They found a split-level with an asking price higher than they had planned to pay, but Claire was smitten with the house, particularly the remodeled kitchen. Their agent negotiated a price that was finally agreed upon, and they took possession a week before their wedding.

They decided their wedding would be as simple as possible.

"Just the two of us," Claire said. "Like they get married in the movies--with a Justice of the Peace."

He concurred, pleased that the matter was resolved without conflict. But the night before the ceremony he had difficulty falling asleep; when he finally dozed off, he dreamt of a wedding quite different from the one planned. He and Claire were standing together under a chuppah, the poles held up by four bearded men in long black gabardine coats, reminiscent of scenes in pre-war Eastern Europe. Claire wore a long white gown, he a dark suit. Standing before them was Kramer's father, prayer book in hand, chanting the Hebrew blessings that formalized their union. As the ceremony drew to an end, his father paused, then switched to English and announced, "If any man can show just cause why these two persons may not be joined together, let him now speak, or else hereafter forever hold his peace."

A door was thrown open followed by a shout, "Stop!" Everyone present turned to look at the intruder. It was Himmelshine in his rumpled suit, dashing forward to the chuppah; he grasped Claire by the arm and then hand in hand, the two of them hurried out of the room.

After a stunned moment, Kramer ran out to the street, just in time to see the couple enter a waiting cab, Claire pulling in the train of her white gown then slamming the door shut as the cab drove off.

Kramer was awakened by the disturbing vividness of the dream. The illuminated numbers on his clock radio indicated the time as being a little after four, but he lay in bed restless, unable to return to sleep. He had almost forgotten about Himmelshine, but now wondered whether his old enemy would pursue him until the end of his days.

They were married in a small room next to the post office in City Hall. The matronly-looking woman standing behind the post office window glanced at her watch when they arrived, then stepped out and led them to the privacy of an adjoining room with a large

American flag in the corner. When the brief ceremony ended, she smiled for the first time and said to Kramer, "You may now kiss the bride."

As they left City Hall and walked to his car, Claire said, "Now we can fuck legally."

Kramer smiled, and then felt compelled to add, "Not according to my mother." He explained that since there was no traditional religious ceremony, Claire was not his wife according to Jewish law.

"Give her time," Kramer said. "She'll come around eventually."

He never mentioned Claire's name during his periodic visits to Philadelphia, although during one unguarded moment as he described recent events, he uttered the words, "my wife." Before he could go on, his mother sharply interrupted him, "She's not your wife; she's your pilegesh," the Hebrew for concubine. Every year before Rosh Hashanah he drove his mother to the cemetery to visit his father's grave. Waiting while she completed her silent communion, he would stand back as she stepped forward to the granite block with its Hebrew and English inscriptions. Each year he saw that she had grown a bit frailer; he knew that soon her name would be inscribed on the half of the stone that was now blank.

There was also an annual visit on Passover, when he joined his mother at the family Seder conducted by his Uncle Morris. When Kramer's father was alive there was always a guest or two at the Seder table, but the Seder remained an intimate family experience. Uncle Morris, however, had children and grandchildren, and the crowded table extended from the dining room to the living room sofa. It was a noisy, joyous evening, despite the restless children and inevitable spilled wine on the white tablecloth. The wine spots always reminded Kramer of the wine stains he had seen on the pages of antique Haggadahs on display in museum Judaica exhibits, the old stains conjuring up the intimacy of similar family gatherings over the centuries.

Uncle Morris was quite observant, insisting on reciting and singing the complete Haggadah service, and by the end of the evening the number of participants had dwindled considerably, the children and their parents having left. Despite her increasing infirmity, Kramer's mother remained until the end of the Seder, Kramer sitting at her side.

Attending the Seder was one of religious issues he discussed with Claire before getting married. They had agreed upon a secular marriage, with no religious observance in the home; each could practice religious rituals alone, but would not impose them on the other. With the coming of children, each child would be free to choose his or her own preference, if any. Kramer and his wife assumed the children would continue their secular orientation.

In negotiating the details of their arrangement, one obstacle was Claire's feeling about Christmas trees.

"It's an old pagan custom," she had insisted. "The tree really has nothing to do with religion." Kramer said that whatever its origins, the tree had become a symbol of the holiday and he could not accept it in his home. Although he was not observant, he refused to participate in the rituals of another faith.

"But it's so pretty and festive -- it's a secular thing, part of the culture. Don't you see trees everywhere, in all the stores, in Jewish stores too?"

The conflict remained unresolved and Kramer had a dream in which he was standing on a dark street, looking at the display window of a furniture store. Two men were decorating a tall Christmas tree. They were in their shirt sleeves, surrounded by boxes of ornaments; each wore a black derby. One of the men stood on a small stepladder near the tree, and the other was handing him decorations. The man on the ladder called out, "Yankel, more tinsel!"

"Enough tinsel already," Yankel said. "Balls you need, Zalman. More balls!"

"What are you talking about? It don't look right. Tinsel!"

The argument continued in Yiddish-accented English as in a vaudeville routine, the two men gesticulating, taking turns going up and down the ladder and stepping back to examine the tree. Finally the man who wanted more tinsel mounted the ladder and draped a single silvery strand on a branch; the tree wobbled under the weight and suddenly collapsed, crashing against the window. Kramer awoke with a start.

The following morning Kramer decided he would not yield on the tree. Finally Claire gave in; he agreed in return to attend her family's annual Christmas dinner and participate in the exchange of gifts. Negotiation and compromise resolved conflicts over religion and other matters as well. All in all, Kramer felt that the interests he and his wife shared outweighed the differences between them. They regularly attended faculty recitals and college theatre performances, and from time to time drove to Philadelphia or New York for an opera or play. With her increasing exposure, Kramer found that Claire relied less on his guidance to the arts.

The last barrier -- the refusal of Kramer's mother to meet Claire--fell with the birth of their first child, Dorothy. Kramer phoned his mother to give her the news; after days of anguished conflict, she could no longer resist the yearning to see her first grandchild. Kramer drove in to Philadelphia and brought his mother to his home. As they entered the house, she carried in two shopping bags with gifts for the baby and Claire met her at the door.

"Hi Mom." She embraced her flustered mother-in-law who dropped her bags on the floor and put her arms around Claire.

"Now let's see the baby," Kramer's mother said, dabbing her eyes.

The attachment to the grandchild grew. Claire had cut back her hours at the bank; Kramer's mother was happy to substitute during emergencies when the usual sitters were unavailable. Claire and Dorothy frequently joined Kramer in his periodic visits to his mother, and when Kramer and his wife went on extended trips--to conventions in San Francisco and Chicago and a summer vacation in Europe--his mother stayed with the child.

The birth of Lance brought complications into the baby sitting arrangement. Kramer's mother continued to sit with the children, but as Lance grew older she found it increasingly difficult to cope with his assertive personality.

"He always says 'No!'" she complained.

Lance told his parents, "I like Mommy's mommy better than Daddy's mommy."

Soon Lance was staying overnight with Claire's family; when Christmas arrived he was enchanted by the tree in their living room and was reluctant to leave for home.

Dorothy began spending holidays and weekends with Kramer's mother, who took her to the synagogue and family religious observances, taught her about the Jewish holidays, how to light and bless the Sabbath candles and how to recite the Four Questions at Uncle Morris's Passover Seder. While Kramer, his mother and Dorothy attended Uncle Morris's Seders, Claire chose not to go, remaining at home with Lance.

With the arrival of winter break at the college, Kramer and Claire joined his colleagues at the annual Christmas party hosted by Tom Boardman. During the conviviality fueled by Tom's ample stock of liquor, talk of holiday plans somehow evolved into a discussion of religion. To everyone's amusement and Kramer's discomfort, Claire, holding her tumbler of Jack Daniel's, announced that Dorothy had become the "Jewish daughter" while Lance was the "Gentile son."

Chapter 18

When Kramer and his son walked together in town or on campus, people often stared and smiled. At times Kramer heard the whisper, "What a beautiful child!" He always smiled in return, for he never tired of these reactions to his son.

He took Lance with him to the college one balmy April afternoon to pick up some papers from his office. When he drove into the parking lot another car pulled up alongside, a red MG. The driver, a young woman who taught piano in the school of music, smiled at Lance, then asked Kramer, "Is that your little boy?"

Kramer nodded and said yes. He took his son's hand, but Lance stood staring at the open sports car, refusing to leave.

"He loves your car," Kramer said.

The woman bent down and asked Lance, "Would you like to sit inside?"

Lance nodded vigorously.

"Then you'll have to tell me your name."

"Lance."

Smiling, the woman opened the car door and Lance got into the driver's seat. With his little hands reaching up to the wheel, he began making his loud car noises. He was wearing his blue blazer, and his blond hair was ruffled by the breeze.

"You're lucky to have such a wonderful little boy," the woman said. She was a new faculty member; he had heard her play Brahms intermezzi at a music faculty recital.

"Yes, I am lucky," Kramer said.

He loved both of his children, but recognized that there was a special quality to his feelings about his son. At times this awareness produced uneasiness and guilt. Kramer wished he could have the same intensity of feeling toward Dorothy. I must be fair, he told himself; it isn't right to prefer one child over another. Yet he knew that he could not change his feelings.

When calling home from a convention or conference, his first question was always, "How is Lance?"

Bringing a gift for Dorothy was easy--she devoured books. Much more thought and effort went into buying a present for his son.

For Lance, cars evoked strong emotion from earliest years. His first toys were cars, pushed on the living room rug to the accompaniment of loud car noises that predated spoken words. The accouterments of cars--miniature gas stations, tow trucks, car trailers--these were the toys to which the child ran in Kiddie City; these were the gifts that elicited cries of delight.

As Lance grew older, the toy cars he preferred were larger more sophisticated--battery powered motors, remote controlled vehicles. When Lance was six he progressed to building classic cars from model kits. Unable to read the instructions, he asked his father for assistance. They sat side by side at the kitchen table, an array of plastic components before them, Lance waiting while his father struggled to make sense out of the blueprints, peering through his thick glasses, straining to find a part that always seemed hidden somewhere in the stamped-out plastic network. Kramer saw the struggle with glue and plastic bits as a grim obstacle course, yet he was eager to join in play with his son.

A relationship was being cemented; Kramer reminded himself, not just plastic components. As he fumbled with the tiny parts, seeking them out, struggling to read the indistinct numbers, Lance grew increasingly impatient with him, urging him on, finally proceeding on his own, ferreting out sections and pieces that eluded Kramer's myopic vision and unskilled fingers.

"I see it!" he would call out, spotting a missing piece. "This is how you do it, Dad," he would say, putting components together.

Soon it was Lance who was the teacher, Kramer the student, uneasy with the reversal of roles and the exposure of his inadequacies. One winter afternoon, when Kramer came home from work, he found his son seated at the newspaper-covered kitchen table.

Lance had just opened a box containing the parts of a new model.

He looked up at his father.

"It's a present, from Uncle Mike."

"Great! If you wait while I put my things away, I'll give you a hand."

"I can do it myself."

The reply was unexpected. Kramer, silent, removed his coat, and then took his brief case up to his study. Sitting at his desk, he was unable to get to work. After a while he berated himself for being foolish; his son's autonomy should arouse pride, not the sadness of loss. But he never offered Lance assistance in model building again.

Chapter 19

Kramer reassured himself that other bridges to his son remained. There were the summers, during which he declined teaching so that the family could be together. Every August they rented the same small white clapboard cottage on Long Beach Island. Claire was a fine swimmer, and in a daily ritual her family watched as she swam out beyond the breaking waves with graceful, rhythmic strokes, her white bathing cap bobbing in and out of view. Kramer and the children stood together, welcoming her as she trudged toward them through the surf, past the other bathers; smiling, she removed her bathing cap as she walked, shaking out her hair with a quick thrust of her head.

"You're back, Mommy!"

Until he was three or four Lance rushed to her and she lifted him into the air, her small lithe body in the single piece red bathing suit displaying surprising strength. For Dorothy, too big to be lifted, there was always a hug. Then hand in hand, father and son took their turn in the water, confronting the incoming waves. At times, after returning Lance to his mother, Kramer would go back in the water for a few minutes, paddling for a short distance, never in a depth above his chest.

But it was in the sand that father and son were happiest. Together they built forts to ward off the waves, forts large enough for Lance to stand in, laughing at each wave as it swirled about in its effort to penetrate the ramparts. As the wall of sand weakened and gradually eroded Kramer and his son hurried to build reinforcements. Both were so engrossed they remained oblivious to the circle of onlookers watching with curiosity and envy the intimate partnership of the blond, copper-skinned boy and his black-bearded father.

Despite repeated sand reinforcements, the fort would eventually begin to crumble, the onrushing waves finally penetrating the center where Lance stood guard. Crestfallen for but a moment,

Lance clambered out of the remains of the fort. "Now let's make a mountain for the ball, Dad."

Together they headed for their blanket, Kramer plodding through the sand behind his son who dashed before him. Dorothy and a classmate she discovered on the beach were playing a game of rummy on a corner of the blanket. Claire, sitting in her low backed yellow canvas chair, looked up from her reading.

"It's time to build a mountain," Kramer announced. Claire smiled and Kramer said, "Come and take some pictures—the camera is under my towel." For a moment Kramer thought of inviting a couple of watching children to join in, but then dismissed the idea-- this was a father and son project. Despite growing fatigue, he got on his hands and knees and began piling sand on the mountain his son had already started. Soon both agreed it was tall enough.

Patting down the sides, they firmed up the mountain, then Lance handed his father the small rubber ball they had brought in the beach bag. With care and concentration, Kramer made a little depression for the ball at the top of the mountain and slowly pushed a descending circular path around the mountain sides. As soon as the path reached the base, Lance extended his hand.

"Let me try it."

"I don't think it's ready."

"Aw, let me try it."

Kramer gave him the ball and Lance placed it on the mountain peak. The ball rolled hesitantly along the path, then came to a premature stop.

"It needs a little more work," Kramer said, widening the path and smoothing out bumps in the sand. "Now try it."

This time the ball rolled swiftly from the top of the mountain, around its slopes, then down to the base.

"Let's make a bridge," Lance said.

Kramer extended the path, building a sand bridge under which the ball rolled before coming to a stop. The mountain completed, Lance called out," Look Mom!"

Claire had gone back to her book, the text for an introductory course in philosophy she planned to take in the fall. She looked up and Lance placed the ball at its starting point, watching it make its gravity-powered descent, again and again. Claire nodded to indicate that she was impressed, and then returned to her reading. Finally Kramer struggled to his feet, walked to the chair beside his wife and sat back to watch their son.

As soon as the films were developed, Kramer mounted the pictures of the summer vacation in a red leatherette covered album-- an album that joined the others on the special shelf in the living room bookcase. At odd moments when alone in the house, or at those rare times during the night when unable to sleep, he would sit in the silent living room and look through the albums of the past, lingering over pictures of his son and the happy times.

Chapter 20

Kramer was awakened by Claire's tugging. Rolling over, he squinted to see the blurry yellow numbers on the radio-alarm, then mumbled, "It's only six-thirty."

"I smell smoke!"

He sniffed, groped for his glasses, and then jumped out of bed. The smell was stronger in the hall. Bare-foot and wearing only his pajamas, he ran to Lance's room but found the bed empty.

Claire was behind him, pulling her robe on. He shouted, "Get Dorothy!" and hurried down the stairs.

Lance was on the kitchen floor beside his giant red fire engine, a Christmas gift from Uncle Mike. Holding the hose in one hand, Lance pumped frantically with the other, sending a stream of water on to a flaming newspaper. Kramer grabbed a bucket from under the sink and began filling it.

Lance shouted, "I'm putting it out!" Holding the half-full bucket, Kramer hesitated as Lance implored, "Dad, don't! I'm putting it out!"

For a moment Kramer was tempted to please his son, and then dismissed the thought as idiotic when he saw flames reaching up from the floor toward a dish towel hanging over the edge of the counter. He emptied the bucket contents on the flames with one thrust; the water splattered over the newspapers, the floor and Lance, who stared disconsolately at the charred and smoking debris.

"I had to do it," Kramer said. "I'm sorry, Lance."

Claire and Dorothy stood in the doorway, watching. Kramer rolled up the wet newspapers and put them in the trash, and then Claire began mopping the floor.

"That fire engine has got to go," she said.

Lance screamed, "No!"

"No? Do you think we're going to let you burn the house down? Now go to your room and get out of those wet pajamas."

Lance began to cry.

"Just a minute!" Kramer said, bending down to examine the fire engine. "Let's compromise. You can keep the fire engine. We'll take the hose off, and give it back to you when one of us is around to watch."

Lance snatched the toy away from his father. "You'll ruin it!"

"All right, you take it off."

Lance pulled on the hose, detached it, and then held it tightly.

Claire said, "Give it to your father."

Shaking his head in refusal, Lance clenched his jaw, tears welling in his eyes.

Kramer said, "I'll let you use it again. I promise."

With drawn-out reluctance, Lance finally handed Kramer the hose, then clutching the top of his pajama pants, he ran out of the kitchen to his room.

Chapter 21

Unlike Lance, whose problems seemed to increase with the passage of time, his sister presented a model of good behavior. Dorothy played the cello in the school orchestra; she memorized poems and was called upon to recite at parties and school assemblies. Throughout the years Kramer and his wife faithfully attended her concerts.

And they were always in the audience when she stepped out from behind the blue velvet curtain on the school stage, alone, a little girl with long brown hair, reciting "The Raven," "Evangeline," or "Hiawatha," in a voice thin yet animated with feeling. A recurrent memory for Kramer was that of Dorothy standing in the middle of their living room, her hands behind her back, reciting before family and guests who sat in hushed silence.

Lance never attended any of his sister's school performances. "I hate that stuff," he said, and his parents gave up on efforts to have him join them. Kramer was proud of his daughter's achievements and took great pains to protect her from Lance's teasing. Trying his best to keep his preference for his son hidden, Kramer couldn't understand why he didn't favor Dorothy, the child who so closely shared his interests and values.

Dorothy was the precocious one, the child who loved to read, who excelled in her studies, who was thrilled by music; was she not like himself? And how unlike him was Lance--robust, impulsive, a boy who gloried in the physical--a stranger to books and the world of ideas. Despite the praise Kramer bestowed on Dorothy for her achievements, Lance's strength, speed, and toughness--all that was primitive and uncivilized in his son and missing in his own childhood--made the boy more endearing to his father.

Dorothy and Claire were in the kitchen baking brownies one Sunday afternoon when the doorbell rang. Kramer went to see who it was. Standing in the doorway was a neighbor, Bill Atwater, a balding man about his own age, and Atwater's son, Jimmy. Kramer gasped; the front of the boy's white sleeveless shirt was stained with blood. The first thought to enter Kramer's mind was that there had been an accident--he would immediately offer to drive Jimmy to the hospital. But then he sensed that the father's mood was not one of urgency but that of grim hesitation.

"Sorry to disturb you, but I wanted you to see this."

Kramer exclaimed, "My God! What happened?"

"Jimmy was in a fight -- with Lance."

"Oh!"

Kramer was stunned, unable to speak. Then his impulse was to rush upstairs, get Lance, and confront him.

"Now wait," Atwater said. "It was a fight--and kids have fights. I just don't want bad feeling between the boys. I'd like this not to happen again."

"Yes," Kramer said. "Please come in."

The boy was hesitant. "Jimmy, you can come in," Kramer said. Atwater put his arm around his son's shoulder and guided him into the living room.

Claire and Dorothy stepped out of the kitchen; Claire gasped at the sight.

"A bloody nose," Atwater explained.

Bloody. The word resonated in Kramer's mind as he went up the stairs, and an image flashed before him: he was a boy, Jimmy's age, walking to school during the winter, after a heavy snowfall. Someone threw a snowball that hit him in the face, smashing one lens of his glasses; his face was cut, there was blood. The snow covered world looked cracked as he struggled to see his way back home.

The door to Lance's room was ajar; as soon as Kramer entered, Lance whispered, "It was his fault! He started it so I let him have it!"

Kramer raised his hand in a calming gesture. "Nobody is being blamed. We just want both of you to make up. Let's go downstairs."

Prompted by Kramer and Atwater the two boys faced each other, shook hands self-consciously and promised not to fight again.

In bed that night, Claire whispered, "I'm worried about Lance. He's only nine and he's acting like a thug.

Kramer could see his son standing tall, strong and fearless, pummeling the Atwater boy. The scene aroused his revulsion. Then later, tossing and unable to sleep, he couldn't dismiss the memory of a violent act of his own; his last encounter with Himmelshine. Once again he felt the sensation of his fist sinking into Himmelshine's spongy belly. With increasing uneasiness, Kramer knew that in some remote region of his being he was proud of his son.

Chapter 22

When the call came, Kramer was in class on an overcast day in February, the scraping sound of campus snow plows filtering into the room. Interrupting the lecture, a student opened the door to tell Kramer he was wanted. Excusing himself, Kramer headed down the hall to the department office; the secretary, her face drawn, handed him the phone.

It was Claire, her voice distorted by sobs. "Dorothy was hit by a car -- she's in the emergency room..."

He asked the secretary to dismiss his class, hurried to the parking lot and drove to the hospital. Fearful that his distress might cause him to lose control of the car, he struggled to focus his attention on the traffic lights and snow covered roads. Yet even after being told by the young, white-jacketed physician as he sat with Claire in the magazine-cluttered waiting room, television blaring, that it was over, that Dorothy was gone, he could feel in the midst of his pain the flash of relief that it was not Lance.

Kramer's mother requested that Dorothy be buried in a Jewish cemetery, and Claire agreed. The grave was not far from that of Kramer's father. In a few weeks' time Kramer's disconsolate mother suddenly grew ill. The deterioration in her condition was rapid, shocking Kramer; she was admitted to the intensive care unit at Einstein Medical Center and in a week, died of pneumonia.

Kramer managed to carry on, impelled by the pressures of duties in the college senate and in his own department. A search for a new college president was under way, and as a member of the selection committee Kramer was locked into a schedule that required his interviewing candidates and showing them around the campus. Another burden he couldn't relinquish was his commitment to serve as coordinator of the department summer school program.

He was also caught up in completing his application for promotion to the rank of full professor before the deadline. These burdens, in addition to his usual duties, formed an academic treadmill that kept him moving through the gray days of sorrow. In bed at night or during the few pauses between compulsory duties, Kramer was haunted by images of Dorothy standing in their living room and reciting "The Raven." At one time, during his lecture in class, he was suddenly conscious of heightened stillness in the room. A memory of Dorothy had intruded, silencing him for a moment; then aware that the class was staring at him and that his eyes were tearing, he hurried to repeat his last sentence and go on.

Claire could not cope with the loss and sank into a depression that seemed deep and endless. She quit her job and college course and remained at home, spending the days in bed, or sitting in the living room in her bathrobe staring at nothing, the gray roots now showing in the stringy hair that hung about her pale face. Kramer took over her duties, preparing breakfast and making sure that Lance got to school on time.

Dinners were mainly frozen Stouffer's or Chinese take-out that he picked up at the Canton House on his way home from the college. The same cleaning woman they had employed for years continued coming in once a week to impose some order on the accumulated debris, working around Claire who remained immobile in a living room chair, oblivious to the vacuum cleaner moving about her slippered feet.

Coming home from the college one afternoon Kramer found his wife in the bedroom getting dressed. He was relieved to see the change, and was about to commend her when she rushed past him to the stairs. "I've got to get out of here," she said.

When Claire didn't appear by dinner time, Lance asked, "Where's Mom?"

"She wanted to get out for a while," Kramer said.

"Does that mean she's better?"

"I hope so."

Kramer spent the evening sitting in the living room, trying to read, all the while listening: for the phone to ring, for the key in the front door, for street sounds that might belong to Claire's approaching car.

Before going to bed, Lance said, "Maybe she went to grandma's house."

The thought of calling his in-laws had occurred to him, but what if they had no idea where she was? There was no point in worrying them. Should he call the hospital? The police? It was premature. When she'd show up, there would be a simple explanation. The delay was not unreasonable; she had been housebound far too long.

It was after two o'clock at night when he felt he had to get to bed, even though not tired. His anxiety mounted as he tossed through the night, snatching fitful bits of sleep. Waking at dawn, a surge of fear coursed through his body when he turned and saw that her side of the bed was empty.

Chapter 23

Everything seemed different, somehow off-center, out-of-kilter, like a picture not properly focused; the feel of the car, the appearance of the street, the stores, and the pedestrians in town. It was because she had been out of touch for so long, Claire realized, a prisoner in her own home, held captive not by bars or a jailer but by the dark paralysis she was now determined to confront. There had been no destination, just the sudden urgent need to break out, to get into the car and go. Yet she was not driving aimlessly but going straight ahead, as though guided by someone, an unseen force, or perhaps just memory.

She was out of town now, on the Pike; the day was sunny, bright, and beautifully clear, a day she should enjoy but could not. The suffocating heaviness was still with her; the passing fields, fences, horse farms, all failed to lift her out of the sea of gloom. Then she saw the motel, remembered it, and realized she had probably been heading there all along.

She turned in at the driveway, and then decided to park on the side, where the car wouldn't be so visible from the road. The lobby was quiet and empty, except for a man scrutinizing some papers at the registration desk. Claire stepped into the bar; a couple was seated in the semi-darkness, bent forward and whispering over a corner table. No one was at the bar. Claire slid on to a stool; the bartender, a youngish woman wearing a white shirt with a red bow tie, put down the glass she was wiping and took Claire's order.

It had been so long, the drink was stronger than she remembered. She sipped it slowly, feeling it move through her body, easing tightness along the way. She had another; the oppressive heaviness was still there, but it seemed more bearable. After a while she decided that the dark room wasn't good for her; she needed sunlight.

As she walked through the lobby to the front entrance past the registration desk, she realized her gait was a bit unsteady--not enough for others to notice, but sufficient to make her exert a conscious control over each slow step. Outside, the brightness was jarring; she paused in the parking area to get her bearings.

A man was standing before her, in uniform, a police officer.

"Are you all right?"

She nodded and tried to smile. He looked strong and well proportioned; she glanced at the badge on his blue shirt, then at the gun in the black holster at his side.

"I'm fine," she said. "Just a bit tired."

He didn't move on, and as he studied her, seemingly uncertain, she was warmed by his solicitude; she reached out and placed her hand on his arm.

"Maybe you ought to lie down," he said.

She smiled again. "Maybe."

"Do you want me to take you inside?"

"Yes."

"To a room?"

"Yes."

"Then just wait here for a minute."

He guided her to a blue Ford parked in front of the motel, opened the door for her and helped her in.

"I'll be right back."

She had never been inside a police car before; a voice startled her and she realized the radio was on, issuing staccato announcements. Soon the officer was back.

"It's all set," he said, showing her a key. "Let's go."

The bland, beige anonymity of the room faded into the background; she was only conscious of him. He stood before her, not moving; he was so much taller than she; looking up she saw that he was studying her, waiting. She ran her hand over his chest; the shirt was so smooth, it seemed tailored to a perfect fit. He removed his blue tie, and then reached down to his belt. She said, "No, let me."

The wide black leather belt held the gun and holster on one side, a polished club on the other.

"Careful," he said. "It's heavy."

She removed the belt, feeling its weight, and rested it gently on a plastic-upholstered armchair, the only chair in the room. She was impatient now, and hurried with the remaining buckle; then reaching in, she felt the warm hardness.

"Mmmm," she said. "Another club."

Chapter 24

At breakfast Kramer tried to be casual, to get the day going without upsetting Lance, when his son asked, "Isn't Mom home?"

Kramer said, "No. She's probably at her parents' house. I'll call there later in the day."

First he tried to reach her at the bank, but was told she hadn't come in. He phoned his in-laws after lunch, hoping he would hear her voice, but it was his mother-in-law who answered the phone.

"I'm calling from the college," he said. "Did you happen to see Claire?"

"No," she said. "Isn't she at work?"

"No."

"Maybe she's home."

"She isn't."

"Well, she's probably out doing some shopping. No need to worry."

"If you hear from her, would you ask her to call me?"

"Sure. Sure."

Putting down the phone, he now felt weak. He scribbled a note canceling his office hours for the day and taped it to his door. Hurrying home, he held on to the wish that Claire would be there, waiting for him. But her car was still missing from the driveway. As he unlocked the front door, he tried to brace himself against the silence and emptiness he knew he would find.

He couldn't decide whom to call first: the police? The hospital? He realized that anxiety was clouding his thinking. In the kitchen he found a clean glass--the sink was filled with dishes--and he gulped a drink of cold water. He decided it would best to call police last. The hospital operator connected him with the Admissions Office.

"Do you have a patient--was someone named Kramer--Claire Kramer admitted today or yesterday?"

"One moment please."

He could hear the thumping of his heart as he waited.

Finally the woman's voice said, "No, we have no one named Kramer."

He thanked her and hung up. With the police number before him, he began dialing, then stopped. The call would be a public acknowledgment that Claire was missing. He was resisting this, looking for steps that would postpone the reality that something terrible might have happened to his wife. He decided to try calling motels. Then his phone rang.

A man's baritone voice asked, "Is this Mr. Kramer?"

"Yes."

"Mr. Kramer... Your wife is here."

"Here? Where? Who is this?" He was shouting and knew that he shouldn't. "I'm sorry." He lowered his voice. "Where is she?"

"At The Five Star, it's a motel on Lancaster Pike, outside of Malvern."

"Is she all right?"

"Yeah, she's okay. Room 206."

"I'll be right there."

He hung up and hurried out of the house to his car.

He wanted to get to the motel as soon as possible. Realizing he was driving at high speed, he tried to slow down; it would be foolish to be delayed by police or an accident. His mind was flooded with questions. Could it be a mistake? Was she really at the motel? If so, was she safe? Did something happen to her?

He was relieved to see Claire's car lined up with the others at the side of the motel. It was an older building with a small enclosed pool near the entrance, empty, its paint peeling. Kramer hurried through the lobby across a worn rug, and then decided to bypass the elevator and head for the stairs. Room 206 was near the end of a dimly lit hall. Kramer ignored the Do Not Disturb sign on the door and knocked. There was no answer.

He knocked again and called out, "Claire?"

There was more silence, and then he heard the hurried sounds of someone moving about in the room. He turned the knob, but the door was locked. His relief at finding Claire now shaded into anger; he couldn't understand why she was shutting him out. Then it occurred to him for the first time that perhaps she was intending to take her life.

Frantic, he was about to run down the stairs to the front desk when the door flew open. Suddenly a tall man stood before him; blue shirt unbuttoned, revolver and a billy club dangling from his waist, he pushed past Kramer and hurried down the hall to the stairs. Stunned, Kramer watched the man disappear, and then stepped into the room to look for his wife.

The window drapes were closed, the only light coming from a weak lamp on a corner table. As his eyes adapted to the semi-darkness, Kramer saw a naked body stretched out on the bed. At first glance he thought it was a young girl, then he realized that it was Claire, on her back, her legs spread slightly with one knee bent.

He rushed to her side. In the dim light, her skin had a yellow glow, and a moist spot glistened on the matted, straw-colored pubic hair. Kramer bent down and put his ear next to her mouth. He could hear her rhythmic breathing; each exhalation vented the smell of alcohol.

He sat on the bed beside her.

"Claire --"

She didn't respond. He covered her nakedness with the bed sheet, took her hand in his.

"Claire -- "

Her eyes flickered open, making momentary contact with him, then closed as she rolled over, turning away. He waited, gently stroking her hair again and again; then he leaned over and kissed her softly on the cheek.

"Claire --"

She mumbled into the pillow, her speech slurred and unintelligible. He searched for her clothes. Her slacks and shirt lay on a chair in a corner of the room. Looking about, he found her shoes near the table, then her bra and underpants on the floor beside the bed.

"Let's get dressed, Claire."

Slipping his arm under her shoulders, he tried to lift her into a sitting position, but as soon as he withdrew support she fell back on the bed. For a few moments he watched her, feeling helpless and not knowing what to do. Finally he pulled back the sheet and slipped her underpants on her feet, then tugged them up to her waist. He fitted the bra on her small breasts, and while reaching behind her back in an awkward embrace to fasten the catch, her eyes opened near his; he saw in them a heavy sadness.

She whispered, "I'm sorry."

"That's all right," he said, as though comforting a child.

He touched his cheek to hers, and then tried again to lift her; this time she sat up. She began sobbing; he held her, murmuring over and over, his glasses misting, "It's all right...it's all right."

Chapter 25

Kramer took his wife to a psychiatrist who tried several anti-depressant drugs, none of which seemed to have noticeable positive effect. Claire was admitted to the psychiatric unit of the county hospital. After two weeks Kramer thought she had improved; her hair was combed and clean, her gaunt appearance faded as she regained some lost weight, and the disheveled look was gone. But he quickly realized that the changes were a cosmetic consequence of better physical care; her dejected mood and profound withdrawal remained. It seemed to Kramer that his visits made no impact on her depression and they left him feeling emptied. He went to see her every day.

Lance's school notified Kramer that his son's absences were excessive and asked him to come in for a conference; Kramer discovered that while he was dropping off his son in front of the school each morning, Lance rarely entered the building.

"Where do you go?" Kramer asked.

Lance shrugged. "Back home, most of the time when you're not there. Or I just walk around."

The next day Kramer accompanied Lance into the school building, leaving after his son's whispered protests.

"They're all looking at us."

"Will you go to your class?"

"Yeah, I promise."

There were no more reports of truancy. One afternoon Lance left his bedroom door open and Kramer saw five new Matchbox miniature cars on his son's desk. When Kramer asked how they were acquired, Lance tried to maintain a direct gaze and said he found them Deception was obvious in the blank contrived look of innocence--Lance was still too young to hide a lie. Kramer sensed that his son was stealing from neighborhood stores, and was reluctant to question further. He didn't want to put Lance on the spot; the thought of trapping his son, making him squirm, was repugnant.

Kramer paused, then said, "Lance, I just want you to grow up to be a good person."

The next day Kramer opened his wallet to pay for lunch in the faculty dining room and was surprised to discover that the twenty dollar bill he thought he had was missing. The cashier waited, as did other faculty members in the line behind him.

Embarrassed, Kramer said, "I guess I'm out of cash. Can I give you a credit card?" With a weak smile, the cashier explained that the dining room wasn't set up for credit cards.

"Let me take that," said a professor from Anthropology, standing behind him in line.

"No no," Kramer said quickly. "But thanks."

Grasping his tray to leave, he told the cashier, "I'll pay next time."

At first Kramer thought he was at fault--he had lost the money, or perhaps he didn't remember spending it. But the incident resulted in his paying more attention to his wallet and the amount of money in it. Before going to bed at night, he routinely emptied his pockets, laying the contents on his bureau. Eventually he determined that money was being removed from his wallet in the morning, while he was in the bathroom shaving.

Kramer was certain that Claire would have confronted Lance at once had she been home and learned of the thefts, yet he hesitated doing so. Finally he decided that the matter could not be ignored. In the evening, after dinner, he knocked on his son's door.

Lance lowered the sound of his television and called out, after Kramer knocked again, "Come in!"

His son was lying in bed, his head propped up with pillows.

"I'd like to talk to you," Kramer said.

Lance turned off the set with his remote.

"There's been some money missing from my wallet."

Lifting himself up on his elbows but still lying on his back, Lance asked, "Are you blaming me?"

"No. I'm not blaming anyone. I'm trying to find out what happened. Do you know anything about it?"

Lance fell back on the bed. "I don't know a damn thing about it. It wasn't me, I can tell you that."

Kramer paused. "Are you getting enough allowance?"

Startled, Lance wouldn't answer at once. He finally said, "No."

Kramer increased the allowance by three dollars a week and no longer left his wallet on the bureau.

Sitting at his bedroom desk grading student papers one evening, Kramer had difficulty focusing. His thoughts detoured repeatedly to the problems he faced: the loss of Dorothy, dealing with his wife's depression, and being troubled by Lance's increasing psychopathic behaviors. Kramer wondered if his own troubled life would ever get better.

Would Claire improve, or was he seeing the first of recurring depressions? Would Lance's dishonesty and thievery develop further into a pattern of hardening criminality? Did it all mean that he himself had made gross errors in his life decisions? Should he have stayed at the rabbinical college? Had he exchanged one bondage for another?

If not for Himmelshine, perhaps he would have married Annamarie and been spared the disappointments with Lance, Claire, and Claire's family. Himmelshine continued to pop into Kramer's thoughts. What had happened to him? Had Himmelshine eventually married Annamarie? Catching himself staring off into space thinking what might have beans, Kramer, disgusted with his self-pity, would eventually force himself to return his attention to the task at hand.

Several days after increasing his son's allowance, Kramer smelled something burning as soon as he entered the house. The foul smell came from the fireplace in the living room. Examining the still smoldering mass, Kramer found the charred remains of photographs. Quickly turning to the bookcase, he saw that one of the red leatherette photo albums was gone. He ran up the stairs to Lance's room--the door was open.

"Why did you do it?" he demanded.

"Do what?"

"The pictures! Why did you burn the pictures?"

"I didn't like them."

"Lance!" Kramer was distraught. "How could you do that?"

"I hated them."

"Pictures of you as a little boy.... They were precious!"

The shock of his son's willful destructiveness kept Kramer tossing for most of the night. He decided that Lance was reacting to Claire's absence and needed much more supervision. With great reluctance, he approached his wife's parents, who agreed to take Lance into their home until Claire left the hospital. Lance stayed for a month, not returning until the day after Claire's discharge.

Chapter 26

The psychiatrist said she was well enough to go home, but Claire wasn't sure. She kept her uncertainty to herself; she felt better and was eager to leave the hospital. Of course the wound was still there, but she had finally been able to talk about Dorothy's death with her psychiatrist and in group therapy. The confinement, the fixed hospital routine, the coerced socialization, the patronizing solicitude of some of the staff, had all become too oppressive. She wanted to be back in her own home with her family.

Entering her house she felt an odd sensation of strangeness, as though the rooms and furniture were in some new arrangement, even though she realized that everything was exactly as she had left it. Going back to work too was odd; the cheerful greetings of her coworkers, the discovery that they had really missed her --it was all so unexpected.

In about a week it seemed that she had not been away at all. Home and work resumed their familiar patterns. She had lost the semester at school, but registered to repeat the course. She continued seeing her psychiatrist, primarily to regulate her medication, which he kept cutting down. What sustained her most was not people, but the determination that she had to go on with her life.

Her husband never spoke of the time he had found her; all she could remember was his struggle to get her into the car. She often wondered if the man she'd been with was still in the motel room when her husband had arrived. Perhaps the man had left. Or perhaps he'd gotten dressed and her husband thought he was a police officer called to the scene, doing his job.

Did the two men speak? She decided never to ask her husband what had happened that day. She thought of the officer from time to time and struggled to recall additional memory fragments of their encounter. It was like watching a surrealistic movie in which another woman was the star, a woman displaying the wild, exaggerated abandon depicted in the orgies of the early silent films. The woman, who looked like herself, was with a handsome man in uniform.

One late afternoon, while driving home from the bank and thinking about what she might prepare for dinner, she was suddenly aware of a flashing light in her rear view mirror. It was a police car; she slowed down, waiting for the car to pass, but it didn't. Uneasy, Claire wondered if she had gone through a light. Finally she was able to pull over to the curb.

The police car drew up behind her, and through her side mirror she saw an officer coming closer. With a catch in her throat that seemed to take her breath away, she realized it was him.

"Hello," he said.

She remained silent, waiting.

"Don't worry; you're not getting a ticket. I just wanted to talk to you. Are you okay?"

She stared straight ahead and finally said, "I'm okay."

"I've been looking for you. I was in the bank a lot of times, but you were never there. I even drove by your house."

He knew where she worked and lived. That surprised her; she wondered what else she had told him. "I'm glad you're okay." He paused, then asked, "Can I see you again?"

She shook her head. The red and blue lights of his car were still flashing in her rear window. She wondered when he would leave.

"I'd really like to see you," he said.

"No." She tried to soften the word. "I don't think it's a good idea."

"Okay. If you ever change your mind, call me at the station. Just ask for Officer Harley."

He hurried back to his car and in a moment was gone. So quickly, she thought; she had expected him to stay longer, to be more persistent.

Chapter 27

Although the memory of Dorothy was always there, they rarely spoke of her. Claire would look away at any mention of her daughter. Fearing a recurrence of his wife's depression, Kramer shared her silence. Even Lance, whose few initial questions about Dorothy were met by his mother's wounded retreat, learned that he was not to speak of his dead sister.

Yet there were constant reminders of Dorothy--her room with its closed door, report card time, summer vacation, the family picture on the mantelpiece. For Kramer, there was an anniversary memorial which he shared with no one. In the year that Dorothy and his mother died, he decided to continue the tradition of visiting the cemetery before the High Holidays.

He always chose a weekday, when it was likely that he'd be the only visitor present. Leaving his car, he walked along the path, at times glancing beyond the sea of gray stones at the wide expanse of meadow--emptiness that would be occupied someday. When he reached the graves of his parents and daughter, he stood still, reading the inscriptions once again, Hebrew and English on his parents' stone, and the English inscription commemorating the brief life of his daughter. Alone, in the midst of the tranquil melancholy of a September afternoon, he recalled the dead as he ran his fingers across the cold surface of each stone.

Renewing the memory of his parents and daughter made him more aware of his aloneness. He was a survivor, the last Jew in his family. He saw himself as a one-way bridge between the generations, spanning past tradition and future oblivion.

The silence was broken by a soft breeze rustling through the leaves of a tree near the meadow. Kramer looked down to the ground and found two pebbles. He placed one on each tombstone, the traditional sign of a visitor. As he did every year, he counted the pebbles already there; they were all his.

Chapter 28

Kramer thought he could date the change in his relationship with Lance to a Sunday afternoon in April, when the family had been visiting Claire's parents. The day was warm and balmy, with a clear blue sky; everyone sat in the cramped living room, waiting for dinner: Claire, Kramer, Lance, Claire's father and her brother Mike. Claire's mother was in the kitchen; she had declined her daughter's offer of help.

Mike, seated in his usual spot before the television set, stood up suddenly in the middle of a beer commercial and announced, "It's too nice a day to be inside." He turned to Lance "Come on, let's go out and have a catch."

Lance rose and followed his uncle out to the front lawn. Soon Kramer heard laughter and shouting.

"No, like this," Mike called, and Kramer realized with a twinge of uneasiness that Mike was teaching his son how to properly throw a ball.

Claire asked, "Do you want to go out with them?"

Her solicitude increased his discomfort. "No. They're doing fine."

The incident remained with him in the days that followed. The next time they visited Claire's family, Mike invited Lance to go out shortly after their arrival, and as if waiting for the opportunity, Lance jumped up and hurried to accompany his uncle. When the two of them were at the door, Kramer called out, "I'll join you!"

Lance threw his father a quick, puzzled look and at once Kramer regretted speaking up, but Mike said, "Sure! That's great!" The front lawn, identical in size to all the others on the block, seemed too small an area for the three of them to have a game of catch. But the space in the larger rear yard was taken up by the hulks of three old Pontiacs, strewn about like beached whales. Lance took up his position on the front lawn near the house, facing his father and Mike, who stood near the curb.

Kramer felt an unexpected rush of anxiety; as his body tensed, waiting for the ball to come his way, he was a boy again, his son's peer rather than his father. Lance threw the ball to him and Kramer thrust out his arms; the ball grazed his fingers and went beyond him. Kramer glanced quickly up and down the street--it would be the final humiliation if he were struck by a car; he ran awkwardly to retrieve the ball, now rolling along the curb.

His heart racing at the unaccustomed exertion, he was back at his position in the yard; Lance observed him in silence while Mike, cheerful, called out, "Practice -- that's what you need--a little more practice."

Kramer threw the ball back to Lance; a slow ball, carefully directed. Lance caught it without difficulty and in a flowing, uninterrupted motion threw the ball to Mike. Mike returned the ball to Lance who, after a moment of hesitation, sent the ball to his father. Kramer, relieved, caught it this time. The sequence was established: back and forth to Kramer, then back and forth to Mike.

Kramer had to run for the ball several more times, pursuing it into the street, his breathing labored, and once or twice his throws were wild, impossible for Lance to catch. But the back-and-forth of the ball between Lance and Mike was smooth, rhythmic, with a grace that Kramer envied.

He wondered if Mike had been an athlete in his youth, the kind of boy who might be chosen as a team captain in gym class. Despite being overweight, his shirt hanging over the edge of his baggy pants, Mike threw the ball with effortless precision. Ten years younger than Claire, Mike seemed like an older brother to Lance.

Kramer was conscious of increasing fatigue when the ball suddenly came at him from nowhere, striking him sharply in his face and knocking off his glasses. The world was now a blur; seized with childhood panic, Kramer squatted on the ground, running his fingers over sidewalk and grass as he groped for the glasses. He found them when the heel of his shoe came down with a crunch.

Slowly he rose. Mike and Lance drew closer, looking as though they were moving under water. Squinting, Kramer tried to examine his damaged glasses when Mike said, "Here--let me look at that."

One lens was shattered; Mike brushed the fragments of out of the frame.

"You have one scratched lens left," Mike said, returning the glasses.

Kramer tried them on with trembling hands. Through the cracks in the single lens he saw his son looking at him, laughing. Like a child publicly exposed, Kramer quickly turned away; he removed the glasses, and Mike said, "We'd better go back in the house."

Chapter 29

At first, Lance would stand beside his uncle and patiently watch as Mike, bent under the hood of a battered Pontiac in the driveway, puttered with some repair or adjustment. Then Lance became a helper. Mike said, "Let me have the Allen wrench," or "the Phillips screwdriver with the wooden handle...." The image for Kramer was that of Mike the surgeon, Lance his operating room assistant. Soon Lance was leaning over the motor alongside his uncle.

Pleased to identify a strength in his son, Kramer said to his wife, "He seems to have mechanical aptitude."

But Claire said, "I don't want him to be a mechanic."

"There's nothing wrong in that. A skilled mechanic is hard to find--it would be a secure, comfortable living."

She looked annoyed. "I want more for him."

"But he's doing so poorly in school. Not everyone has academic interests. Being a mechanic --"

Claire cut him off. "I want Lance to go to college, whatever it takes. He has the ability--he only needs the motivation, that's what everyone has been telling us for years."

She did it, rising from the bottom on the academic ladder; Lance could do the same. Kramer, seeing no point in a quarrel, remained silent. But he believed his view was the realistic one, acquired by sitting with Lance year after year at the dining room table after dinner, in the joint effort to complete the boy's daily homework assignment. The table would be piled with Lance's books and a sloppy array of papers spilling out of his loose leaf binder. Kramer's task was to support and urge, short of provoking resistance in his son, who faced the nightly ordeal with sullen distaste and confusion. When pushed too far Lance would stand up suddenly and fling his algebra text on the table with a shout, "I can't stand this shit!"

He would run up to his room to watch television, leaving the homework undone. Then came the inevitable sequence of cut classes, failing report cards, and finally the calls from the school to attend another conference. Kramer, feeling himself to be the defendant, would sit in a cramped room at a small table with the prosecution: principal, disciplinarian, guidance counselor and teachers. As damning reports and test results were read before the group, he found himself speaking up as Lance's ally, trying to convince the others that his son was really a bright, worthwhile boy.

At home Kramer persisted in his efforts to help Lance, but the tension around schoolwork increased. There were more explosive departures from the table; Kramer feared growing damage to his relationship with his son. "We're getting nowhere," he told Claire.

"What'll we do? We just can't let him fail."

"How about a tutor?"

"We tried that. He hated her."

"If we got a man--someone he might like ..."

Claire shook her head. "I'll give it a try myself."

Kramer nodded in agreement. "Maybe that's the way to go. Take turns. This is too draining for one of us alone."

He remembered the nights they spent when Lance was a baby, cranky, restless, and crying endlessly--they took turns then too, holding him, pacing in the darkness.

When he wasn't preoccupied with courses, research, publications and committees, Kramer ruminated over his son. One of their few remaining points of contact was Lance's interest in board games. Over the years, Kramer participated in his son's evolution from Candy land through cards, checkers, Battleship and Monopoly. On rainy weekends in particular, Lance, tiring of his models and television, might still turn to his father. "Let's have a game of Monopoly, Dad."

Kramer always seized the opportunity. Lance's attention, so restless and easily lost, would be more focused in play. He liked playing War and Battleship; as they sat at the dining room table, Lance grew more animated with the rising excitement of a game, particularly if he were winning. A victory for Lance produced an elation that delighted Kramer. However, when he lost, Lance would withdraw from the table, frowning and petulant. To spare his son, at times Kramer would fake a loss.

Claire noticed this one afternoon, and when they were alone she accused, "You threw that checker game, didn't you."

"He was upset," Kramer said. "I had just beaten him in two games."

"Isn't it bad to fake it that way? How will he learn to take real disappointment? He'll grow up thinking everything comes easy, that you don't have to work hard to achieve."

It was obvious that she was right. Kramer realized he had been protecting his son almost unconsciously, without much thought. He resisted the temptation to fake a loss when they played checkers again, and in a devastating move, Kramer jumped three men and won the game. Lance sat for a moment of stunned silence. Then, his eyes rimmed with tears, he rose from the table, angry at himself, his father, the world.

"I'm not gonna play anymore," he said. Kramer tried to comfort his son and offered to take him to a movie, but Lance would not be appeased. When Claire reached out to him, Lance pulled away shouting, "Leave me alone!" It was Kramer's last checker game with his son.

The evening homework sessions seemed to go better with Claire.

"I'm firmer with him than you are," she told Kramer. "He knows I mean business."

They decided she alone would work with Lance; Kramer volunteered to free the time for her by cleaning up after dinner. But after a week of progress Lance began to display a failure to comprehend even the simplest of tasks presented by his mother.

"You know that," she insisted. Over and over she reviewed elementary problems in Arithmetic, easily answered questions in

History. But the material she covered was not retained. Lance didn't bolt from his chair; in response to her insistence he sat still, but displayed a blankness of expression and an opacity of mind that infuriated her.

"You're just not paying attention!" she shouted. "You're not listening!"

Kramer could hear her in the kitchen as he quietly loaded the dishwasher.

Later, Claire asked, "Is he really that stupid? I can't believe it."

"It's passive-aggressive behavior," Kramer said. "Instead of exploding, he's playing dumb."

"I'm not giving up."

But in a few days she did, directing some of her exasperation and anger at her husband.

"You're the expert, for heaven's sake. The psychologist. Can't you figure out something that will work?"

He explained that the problem was one of motivation, that Lance found nothing gratifying in school achievement.

"Can't we make it gratifying?"

"We could try behavioral techniques--a reinforcer, a reward."

"What can we reward him with? He has everything!"

One afternoon when Kramer came home, as he turned the key in the front door lock he was surprised to hear barking. A brown and black dog greeted him, yelping and jumping up on its hind legs. Lance was trying to hold the dog back by the collar.

"What's going on?" Kramer asked.

Gripping the collar with one hand and patting the dog with the other, Lance attempted to calm the animal.

"He's happy to see you."

"Whose dog is it?"

His son was now on the floor, playing with the dog who was wagging his tail and ignoring Kramer.

"He followed me home from school. Maybe he belongs to no one."

"No one?" Kramer had taken off his coat and now, bending over the dog, he reached for the collar. "He has a tag. Let's see what it says." Trying to keep the dog still, Kramer grasped the silver colored tag, squinted, and then called out, "Skippy. That's his name. Let's see what's on the other side."

Lance held the dog as Kramer went on, "Sullivan. There's a phone number. We'll call and tell the Sullivans we found Skippy."

"Aw, can't we keep him?"

"Keep him? No, we can't. He's a lost dog--he belongs to someone. I'm sure they're worried about him. And I'm sure he wants to go home."

"But he followed me."

Kramer laughed. "We can't keep him. He belongs to someone else."

"Can't we let the dog decide where he wants to live? He followed me--he didn't have to. Maybe he wants another home."

By now Claire arrived and again the dog ran to the front door, barking wildly. Lance pulled the dog back, letting his mother in.

"What's that dog doing here?" she demanded.

"His name is Skippy. Isn't he great?"

"He followed Lance home," Kramer said. "The owner's number is on the tag. I was just about to call."

"Let's keep him, Mom!"

"Keep him? Are you out of your mind?"

"But he wants to stay here! He followed me!"

"Dan, go ahead and call. That's all we need--somebody's dog."

Lance began to cry and Kramer put his arm around his son's shoulder. The dog was barking now, agitated by the pandemonium around him. Kramer went to the bedroom to make the call.

The dog's owner claimed him an hour later, with effusions of apology and gratitude. As soon as they left, Lance demanded a dog of his own. "Absolutely not," Claire said. "And stop whining."

"Maybe we can find a way," Kramer said.

"What are you talking about?"

Watching his parents, Lance suddenly grew quiet. He followed them into the kitchen, where Claire began preparing dinner.

"He really wants a dog--it could be a powerful motivator. We might be able to work out a program that would strengthen his school performance."

Lance was enthusiastic and Claire's objections weakened. Kramer devised a contingency management program. If Lance passed at least three major subjects on his next report card, they would buy him a dog within a week. To pass, he would have to change his homework habits. "We'll help you," Kramer said.

"Every day you'll report to me or your mother what your homework assignment is. After dinner you'll get to work--one of us will be available if you need any help."

Lance was eager to start the program and it was initiated that evening. After three days, Lance said he had no homework. The following evening he said he wasn't feeling well. His enthusiasm evaporated by the end of the week, and the dog, unearned, was soon forgotten.

After showering Kramer put on his bathrobe. Reaching for his new glasses, he discovered they were gone. Frantic, he brought his face down close, but the shelf in the mist-filled bathroom was bare. His fresh clothes were laid out on the bed. He dressed quickly and through shadows headed for the back door; he could make his way out of the house with eyes closed. The yard was bright and hot in the midday sun. Lance shouted to his new friend Andy. Were they playing catch? Drawing closer, Kramer saw that it wasn't a ball they were tossing but his glasses, sparkling in the sunlight.

"My glasses!" he shouted, running to Lance. "Give me my glasses!"

Grinning and standing tall and handsome, Lance waited until Kramer reached him, and then threw the glasses to Andy. Then

Andy waited, and at the last minute threw them back to Lance. Running back and forth between them, Kramer felt tears of frustration rising; it was the same as when he was a child and playmates pulled off his hat, refusing to return it, laughing as they threw it into the air, back and forth...

Claire shook him awake.

"You were crying!"

Groping in the dark, he reached for the night table. His glasses were there.

Chapter 30

It was Lance who precipitated the first religious crisis in their marriage. When he was a young child, Lance seemed to adapt easily to the different holidays celebrated by his grandparents. At Christmas and Chanukah, there was a tree in one home and candles in the other, two holiday dinners, two sets of gifts. To the surprise and relief of his parents, Lance never asked questions about the difference.

So when Claire approached her husband on a December evening after Lance had gone to bed, her whispered "Can I talk to you?" took him aback.

The subdued tone of her voice, the grim look that meant something serious was afoot, compelled him to put down his paper. She signaled with a finger that he accompany her to the den, a rare gesture indicating that what was to be said had best not be heard by anyone else. With the foreboding aroused by such an invitation, Kramer followed his wife and quietly closed the door behind him. Claire leaned forward in the recliner.

"It's about Lance. Upstairs, before going to bed, he told me he wanted a Christmas tree."

Silently absorbing the impact of the unexpected request, Kramer now realized that their prenuptial discussions had dealt only with their relationship; the impact of a child's arrival wasn't included. While the question of circumcision did come up when Lance was born, this was dealt with as a medical issue, with Claire in favor of the procedure for reasons of health. Now they faced, for the first time, an unanticipated development that fit into the "if something else turns up, we'll resolve it by discussion" category.

Kramer asked, "What did you say to him?"

"I said I'd talk to you about it."

Kramer wondered why his son had chosen to make the request when alone with his mother. Did the boy anticipate his resistance?

He asked his wife, "What do you think?"

Claire shrugged. "I know it's contrary to our agreement, but why not?"

She paused; he saw that she was studying his face. "You don't seem happy about it," she said.

"It's not rational, I know. It's an emotional thing. It would be difficult for me to accept a Christmas tree in my home."

She hesitated, the way she did when approaching sensitive ground, not wanting to precipitate ill feeling if it could be avoided.

Finally she asked, "Why would it be difficult? I'm not challenging you--I just want to understand."

He acknowledged the reasonableness of her question with a nod. "I know that it's not really a religious ritual," he said, "that it's a pagan custom pretty much secularized in our culture." Then, in response to the serious, attentive look on her face, he searched for a comic touch to ease the growing tension. "There were no Christmas trees in Bethlehem."

She smiled. "Then why not have a tree? For Lance?"

"It would just make me very uncomfortable. I don't know why."

She dropped the matter, but he knew it would come up again. Time, rather than easing the pressure, would magnify it as they drew closer to the holiday.

Several days later, after Lance had gone to bed, Kramer was in the study reading a journal when his wife stepped into the doorway.

"Can I interrupt?"

"Sure."

"I've been thinking about the tree. I can understand how you feel. It's not part of your background--it's something you've never had. And even though you recognize it's now a secular thing, you probably feel there's something religious about it--sort of a symbol of Christmas. And that makes it a religious ritual-- something we agreed not to have in our home."

"Yes," he said, appreciating her recognition of his feelings.

"If it were just me," she went on, "I'd agree with you. There'd be no problem. But the fact that it's Lance–I guess that makes the situation a little different. He keeps asking me about a tree. Could we get one, and why not? Has he approached you at all about this?"

While not intended, the question had the impact of an indictment; he had to answer no, thus acknowledging distance from his son and the possibility of failure as a parent.

"Well, I don't have to tell you this," she said, "but he's on the edge of adolescence. I guess he'll be dealing with identity issues. Maybe the request for a tree is part of that--an attempt to work out his identity."

Kramer hadn't thought of this. His wife, restrained and soft-spoken, seemingly supportive of his feelings, had moved closer to another region of vulnerability--his concern for the emotional well-being of his son.

Claire leaned forward. "Over and over you've said how you wanted to improve your relationship with Lance. Here's a chance to do something that will please him."

Kramer thought of his relationship with his own mother and father. How would they have felt if upon visiting his home they discovered a Christmas tree in the living room, with the glittering decorations, flashing lights and pervasive smell of evergreen? Would his parents try to hide their emotions, not wanting to offend?

Suddenly he remembered the Biblical prohibition against the worship of the Asherah, sacred wood goddess of the Canaanites. A wave of uneasiness seized him; irrational as it might be, the thought occurred to him that he was being pressed into an ancient act of idolatry.

"Maybe there could be a compromise," Claire said. "A small tree. An artificial one, if you prefer."

He tried to remain calm, to respond to her arguments with reason. It was the principle, not the size, he told her. And even if he agreed to a tiny tree, a new tradition would be established and the tree would grow bigger over the years.

"I just can't do it. Please Claire, don't push it."

He was rarely angry with her, and when he was, his wife preferred to withdraw rather than fight back. Silent, she turned away and left the room.

She had little to say to him in the days that followed, but worse was the look in his son's eyes and the feeling of growing estrangement. The hushed remoteness of both his wife and son persisted, preoccupying Kramer, intruding into his thoughts at odd times during the working day. Finally, lying in bed two nights later, sensing that his wife was awake and wide-eyed beside him, he broke the silence.

"Claire?"

"Yes."

"You're awake?"

"Yes."

"Go ahead, get a tree."

She didn't move nor speak. He could feel her incredulity in the darkness.

"Get a tree," he repeated. "And ask Lance to go with you. Tell him I said it was okay."

Tossing in bed, he was unable to fall asleep. Then giving up, he quietly left the bedroom and went to his study. It was after five when he awoke, surprised to discover that he'd slept at his desk. It was too late to go back to bed; rather than wake Claire, he went down to the kitchen to prepare an early breakfast.

Kramer was in his study several days later when the tree arrived--he could hear Claire and Lance moving it about in the living room, arguing about its location, and then setting it on its stand. He thought he should step out and help them, but was unable to leave the study; it was as though he were a child hiding behind a closed door, fearful of meeting a stranger who had just entered the house.

Perhaps he could remain at his desk, surrounded by his books and files, and just wait it out. It would not be forever; eventually his wife and son would complete whatever had to be done to the tree and they would leave. Then he would emerge.

There was a knock on his door. He rose quickly; it was Lance.

"Dad, do you want to see the tree?"

His son waited. Finally Kramer followed him into the living room. The tree, in a corner near the stereo, dominated the room with its large, unfamiliar presence; it seemed to be standing there expecting him, its branches extended, its evergreen aroma beckoning.

"We're going to decorate it now," his wife said, pointing to the unopened boxes on the floor--lights, tinsel, brightly colored ornaments. It was an invitation for him to participate, to join in a new family ritual, but he stood there, knowing he could not be part of this. He had to leave, quickly, but didn't know how to escape. They were observing his awkward silence, waiting for some response.

"I have to go," he blurted at last. He hurried to the closet, got his coat and called out at the door, "I'll be back in time for dinner."

He could not get accustomed to it. The tree was not his, but an alien intruder belonging to his wife and son. He found himself avoiding it, staying out of the living room; when compelled to be present, he felt that he was no longer in his own home. He hid in the study, preparing courses for the spring semester, working on his research. He waited, counting the days.

Then at last it was over. Walking home on a January afternoon he passed three or four trees lying beside trash cans, looking like tattered casualties on a field of battle. When he reached his own house he saw the tree, fallen and abandoned on its side at the curb, shorn of its stature and glory, waiting to be picked up in the morning. He hurried into the house, hoping it would be easier the next year.

Chapter 31

Claire stood in the kitchen, phone in hand. Lance was at Andy's house and her husband had a late afternoon class. Home alone, she wanted to make the call, yet couldn't. She remained standing for a while then hung up and walked away, thinking that her hesitancy must have some meaning. Perhaps this wasn't the right time, perhaps she really didn't want to see him. Perhaps she was afraid.

It was time to be planning summer vacation at the Jersey shore, but Lance had surprised them by refusing to go away, preferring to stay home, swimming in the Y pool and spending time with his friend Andy.

She rinsed a few dishes in the sink, placed them in the dishwasher, thinking how quiet the house was, how dull. With the coming of vacation time there would only be more boredom for company. She thought of the police officer and went to the phone again. The upstairs phone in the bedroom was the one she preferred, but then someone might come into the house without her knowing it. In the kitchen she could end the call as soon as she spotted her son or husband at the door.

Again she hesitated, holding the phone, listening to the dial tone, finally convincing herself she had to call. The boredom was becoming intolerable--it could slide into depression. And as the boredom deepened, so did her restless yearning for excitement.

She dialed the number, and as she heard the first ring it occurred to her that he might not be there at all but out on duty; she would be asked if there was a message—would she please leave her name? The prospect frightened her and she quickly hung up.

At first there was relief; she was spared. But then the absurdity of her behavior struck her. If she didn't try, how would she ever reach him? She could call and decline giving her name when asked. Just say, "That's all right--there's no message--I'll call again."

Her hand was unsteady as she lifted the phone, this time determined to complete the call. When she asked for Officer Harley, the voice said, "Just a minute." She felt her heart race; maybe he was there after all.

"Hello?"

She cleared her throat. "Officer Harley?"

"Yes."

"Hi. How are you?"

There was silence, then, "Who is this?"

"Me. Claire."

"Claire? Claire! Hey--I'm glad you called. How are you?"

She was about to answer Fine but instead heard herself say, "Bored."

"That's too bad."

"Yes it is. I don't know what to do about it."

"Let's get together. I have some ideas."

"Okay."

They agreed on a time.

"The same place? He hesitated, but finding a different, unfamiliar motel would be a complication.

"Okay." Then she added quickly, "And please, no liquor."

"Sure."

They had arranged for him to arrive first but when Claire pulled into the parking area of the motel she couldn't find him. She drove around the side to the rear, then along the other side; there was no police car. She parked and waited; perhaps he was delayed. Then a car pulled up in the space beside her, a red Chevy, and a man stepped out. He wore jeans and a white turtle neck--at first she didn't recognize him.

"You drove right by me," he said.

"Where's your uniform?"

"I'm off duty."

"I want you to wear it."

"Okay, next time."

"No. I've got to have you wear your uniform."

"Do you mean it?"

"Yes."

She saw that he didn't understand. It was an essential part of the excitement. The uniform.

"Can you get it?"

"That means going home," he said.

"I'll wait."

Chapter 32

When Kramer first met Lance's friend, the impression was a negative one: Andy's teeth were crooked and stained, and with his camouflage shirt and crew cut hair he looked like an adolescent soldier. Claire was outspoken in her dislike.

"He has a sneaky smile."

The two boys were out of the house most of the time, but when indoors they played cards and video games in Lance's room. Claire could hear their bickering and excited shouts coming from behind the closed door.

"They're so secretive--why should the bedroom door always be closed?" she asked Kramer.

"That's how adolescent boys are," he said, recalling the sexual jokes whispered during his teens while he and his friends furtively eyed adults who might overhear.

"It's a closeness that excludes adults--don't let it upset you."

Kramer and Claire tried to be casual about Lance's friend; they were rewarded with increasing information about Andy, the subject of periodic announcements at the dinner table.

"When Andy was a kid, his father left the family. Nobody knows where he is."

"How does his mother manage?" Claire asked.

"She works. She's a waitress."

They ate in silence, and then Kramer said, "It must be tough for Andy, not having his father."

"He doesn't care. In fact, he's happy he's gone. His father beat them."

"He beat Andy and his mother?" Claire asked.

"Yeah, and his sister too. He has an older sister. She's a little retarded."

Kramer started to share his wife's uneasiness about Andy when they learned that the boy's mother frequently had to take off from work and go to Andy's school because of his truancy. When summer vacation ended, Lance announced that Andy was quitting school permanently. "He just hates it. His mother sees no point in forcing him to go."

"What will he do all day?" Claire asked.

"I dunno. He's supposed to clean up the house. And watch his sister--she's home too. He just hangs around, watches TV, and goes into town."

"That doesn't sound good," Claire said.

"He hates cats. He really does. He puts them in the oven."

Claire dropped her fork. "What?"

Lance laughed. "Yeah, ever since he was a little kid. If he finds a cat he puts it in his oven and turns it on. He likes to hear the cats scream."

"How horrible!"

Lance laughed. "He's a little crazy, but he's fun."

The laugh had the depth and resonance of adulthood, taking Kramer by surprise as he suddenly noticed that his son's voice was changing. The blond hair had grown darker, the face had lost its softness, and Lance's shoulders and chest were fuller. It had all been gradual, but the impact coming now, with the horrific story of the cats, gave Kramer the chilling sensation that this was not the son he adored, but a stranger.

"That doesn't sound like someone you should have as a friend," Kramer said. "I don't think you should see him."

"Lance -- please stay away from that boy," Claire said.

Lance grimaced and said nothing.

With the beginning of a new semester, Lance had to repeat several failed subjects and Kramer's thoughts returned once again to the problem of motivating his son. Claire's tutoring and the reinforcement program he'd devised had been sloppy. The reward of a dog was too distant; he had failed to include successive reinforcement of small steps in his son's study behavior and homework.

As the school year progressed, Kramer berated himself for not working harder to help his son, but other concerns were competing for his time and attention, concerns that he could not push aside. A paper he'd submitted to a journal had to be revised. There was a deadline for the manuscript of his second book. After finally achieving promotion to Full Professor, he felt obligated to accept the chairmanship of the department curriculum committee.

He came home late one evening from a meeting of the faculty senate and found Claire waiting for him in the living room. He was surprised to see that Lance was still up, sitting in the Queen Anne chair, silent.

"We've got a problem," Claire said. She pointed to a box on the coffee table; it had the picture of a red racing car on the side. "Lance had this in his room. A car model, radio controlled. He admitted that he and Andy took it--stole it--from the hobby shop in the shopping center."

Kramer's heart sank. He glanced at his son, hoping for a denial or explanation, but Lance turned away.

"At first he said he found it, and then he said he bought it. I finally got the truth out of him. I think he should bring it back tomorrow, right after school. I'll be at work. Can you take him?"

Kramer reached into his pocket for his appointment book. He could free up some time in the afternoon.

Lance asked, "Do I have to go? Can't you drop it off for me, Dad?"

"No," Claire said. "You have to return it--and apologize to the store owner."

"Why?" Lance's voice cracked. "I'm not apologizing to anybody. Why can't I pay for it and keep it?"

"Because that's too easy," Claire said, her anger rising. "You've got to learn a lesson here...this mustn't happen again."

Claire glanced at Kramer, looking for his support, but he remained silent, paralyzed, and unable to join her against his son.

"I could say I forgot to pay for it--which I came back with the money." Again the voice cracked. "I just forgot, that's all."

Claire was glaring at Kramer; he felt compelled to speak up.

"I wish we could make it easier for you, Lance. But your mother is right. The car was taken--you have to return it."

"Why?"

"Because we want you to grow up to be a good person. We're concerned about the sort of man you'll become. We're concerned because we love you..."

"Love -- Shit!" Furious, Lance jumped up from his seat. Muttering under his breath, he ran up the stairs to his room and slammed the door.

For the remainder of the evening Claire avoided looking at Kramer. As they undressed for bed, he said, "You're angry at me. What's the matter?"

There was fury in her eyes as she turned to him. "You know what's the matter. Why weren't you on my side? When I needed you, you just sat there. Do you expect me to carry this all by myself?"

The intensity of her anger surprised him; he reached out to her and she pulled away, getting into bed and turning her back to him.

"I'm sorry," he said. "You're right; I should have been tougher with him. But it's hard for me..."

Her shoulders began to shudder and he realized she was crying. Then her weeping grew audible. "I don't want him to be a thief...a failure..."

He reached out again and she didn't respond. He turned her toward him; her body was limp as he tried to comfort her. He held her, pressed her damp face to his, and for a moment he didn't think of his son. She remained distant, inert. Her coldness pained him, yet he understood it; as a father and husband, he had disappointed her. Claire's eyes were closed; she remained motionless, as though he weren't there. He stared at her for a while, then leaned over and whispered into her ear, "I love you."

132

It was a late morning for Kramer. When he came downstairs for breakfast, Claire had already left for work and Lance was zipping up his leather bomber jacket.

"Dad--please take it back for me."

They were both in the living room, looking down at the box on the coffee table with its picture of a red racing car.

Kramer shook his head slowly. "I just can't do that, Lance. I'll go with you to the store, after you come home from school."

Lance gave an imploring look. His face had grown more angular, losing the roundness of childhood. He would grow into a handsome man, Kramer thought.

"Come on, Dad. Take it back for me."

Kramer was silent, struggling with the temptation to yield. His son would be grateful; it might draw them closer.

"If you take it back, I'll never do it again. I promise. I swear."

Kramer hesitated, and then said, "You'll be late. We'll talk more about it when you come home from school."

Through the living room window Kramer watched his son hurry down the street. Then later in the morning, standing at the front door and about to leave, Kramer glanced at the box on the coffee table and suddenly decided to return it. Driving to work, the box at his side, Kramer could see the pleased surprise on his son's face as he told him the good news.

He came home early, to be there when Lance returned from school. He picked up a journal, became engrossed in an article, and when finished realized Lance was late. More time passed and Kramer began to worry. Thoughts about surprising Lance were replaced by concern that something might have happened to his son, the worst case being an accident, like the one that snuffed out Dorothy's life. Unable to read he began pacing about the living room, listening to the local all-news radio station. A little before six o'clock Claire arrived, carrying a bag of groceries. He took the bag from her and she followed him into the kitchen.

"Where's Lance?"

"I don't know."

She turned to him, surprised. "Hasn't he come home?"

"No."

She glanced at Kramer and said, "Don't worry. Lance can take care of himself. He probably didn't want to return the model. He'll show up."

"You seem pretty sure of it."

She went to the phone, still wearing her coat, and called her mother.

"Hi Mom," she said. "Listen, is Lance there?"

Kramer stood, waiting. She turned to him, her hand on the mouthpiece. "He's at my mother's." Claire resumed her conversation. "Yes. That's okay. We'll be over later."

She hung up. "He took a bus from school. He's staying there for dinner -- I told her we'd be over later to pick him up." She paused. "My mother says he wants to stay there--he doesn't want to come home."

"That's ridiculous."

"She told him he belongs home with his family."

Kramer was uneasy. "I would have been happier if your mother called us as soon as he arrived."

"Look. He's her grandchild. Maybe all she knows is that he stopped by for a visit."

Claire failed to notice that the box was gone from the coffee table. As they left the house, Kramer decided he would tell her later that he had returned it. Now was not the time. They arrived around 7:30, after his in-laws had finished dinner; Kramer didn't want a scene while everyone was still seated at the table. Mike came to the door with a cheery hello. Lance, on the couch watching television with his grandfather, gave his parents a momentary glance then turned his attention back to the set.

Waving from his chair, Claire's father called out, "This is a great game."

"Come on, Lance," Claire said. "We're going home."

Lance, hesitant, glanced at his uncle and grandfather. Then Claire's mother came in from the kitchen.

"Leaving already?"

"We've got to go," Claire said. "Lance has homework. Thanks for giving him dinner."

"Our pleasure."

"Let's go, Lance," Claire said.

Lance didn't move. "Are you going to make me apologize?"

Kramer said, "We'll talk about that later."

Lance shook his head. "I'm not coming if you're gonna make me go and apologize."

Claire's mother, wiping her hands on her apron, smiled and asked, "What's this all about? What did he do?"

There was silence, then Claire said, "Tell your grandmother, Lance."

Lance lowered his head and the silence was finally broken by Kramer. "We don't have to talk about that now. We'd better leave." He put his arm about his son's shoulder. "Come on, Lance."

With a grimace Lance quickly pulled away and headed for the door. They got into the car and Kramer was unable to shake off the sting of his son recoiling from his touch. Claire and Lance were talking, their voices rising at times. Driving in silence, his body still feeling the memory of his son's revulsion, Kramer heard their voices but not the words. Did Lance really dislike him so? The thought had never occurred to him before, but now it gnawed at his soul.

He tried to ease the pain by telling himself that he was overreacting to a passing expression of anger. Lance did not yet know he had been spared the humiliation of returning the model car; the anger would fade the moment he realized his father had come to his rescue.

As soon as they entered the house Lance called out, "Where's the car?"

Kramer said, "I returned it."

"What?" Claire swung around, staring at him. "You returned it?"

"Yes. Lance asked me to this morning. He promised it wouldn't happen again."

Her mouth open, Claire looked at him for a few unbelieving moments, then quickly turned away and hurried into the kitchen. Kramer glanced at his son, hoping for some acknowledgment, perhaps an expression of thanks, but Lance shrugged and went upstairs. Kramer stood alone in the living room. He finally decided against trying to explain to Claire; he had blundered enough for one day. With heavy steps he went to his study, closing the door behind him.

Chapter 33

She saw him every Thursday afternoon. Her husband knew she couldn't be reached, that it was not one of her work days; that she was driving about, probably tending to her many errands.

The motel had a worn, shabby air, yet the rooms–they had used several, she'd lost count--were clean and well maintained. Claire loved the freshness that always greeted them when he unlocked the door: the made bed, vacuumed carpet, furniture-- although cheap--always dusted. And the fresh towels and wrapped glasses in the bathroom. All prepared by an invisible host just for their festive arrival.

"It's an oasis," she said to Tony.

"What do you mean?"

"Like an island. A place completely disconnected from the rest of my life--away from all the pressures, the worries about job, family, school..."

She learned that he was married, had two children, and was happy with his work. There had been many women. And like the spring in an oasis, he nourished her, making her aware of the hunger she'd been harboring for so long. He continued to surprise her with the responses and sensations he could elicit from her body.

"Tony, you're a virtuoso."

"What's a virtuoso?" he asked.

"A great artist--a musician. You know exactly how to play my body--as if it were an instrument. A cello. How did you learn that?"

He laughed. "Practice."

She wondered if she was reacting to the uniform, the secrecy, or the allure of the forbidden. They all added to the excitement and pleasure, but there was no doubt in her mind that Tony was good in bed, certainly better than her husband.

His one talent was physical; the little he had to say was mostly in response to her questioning. And then his answers were simple, concrete and monosyllabic. Almost always she talked and he listened.

As the weeks went by she adapted to his dullness, and came to the conclusion that she needed two men, one for her body and one for her mind. Seeing Tony one afternoon a week was just right--prolonged contact would be tedium. Claire knew she could never live with Tony--between orgasms, what would she do? And her husband Dan, despite his deficiencies, was not a bore. Although she couldn't satisfy all of her needs with one man--could any woman? She had the good fortune to find contentment with two.

After six months he remembered the anniversary of their first meeting and bought her a gift, a silver pin. He told her that he loved her and wanted to marry her.

She shook her head. "No, Tony. That's very sweet, but we're both married already."

"We can get divorced."

"That's not a good idea."

"Why not?"

"You have your wife, your children; I have my husband and son."

"I'll give up my wife for you any day."

"I can't leave my husband, Tony."

"Why not?"

"I just can't."

"Do you think he'll give you trouble? I'll take care of him."

"No, Tony," she said, frightened. "Don't you dare hurt him. Don't even think of it."

"Okay."

"I'd never forgive you."

"Okay, okay. Do you love him?"

She hesitated, and then said, "Yes."

"How can you love him and fuck me?"

She looked up at him and drew her fingers across his cheek in a soft caress.

"Answer me," he demanded. "How can you do it? How can you love him and fuck me?"

She smiled. "I manage."

Chapter 34

At night Claire frequently shut herself in the bedroom to study at her desk. Through the closed door Kramer could hear the reverberating taped voice of the professor whose lectures she had recorded in class. At times an obscure phrase was repeated monotonously as she played it over and over.

When the last course was completed and Claire finally earned her BA, Lance and her parents were in the audience on commencement day, a warm May afternoon. Kramer, seated with the gowned faculty, watched as she stepped across the stage to receive her diploma from the college president. Kramer's eyes met hers as she walked down the aisle back to her seat and they shared a private smile.

To celebrate, Kramer insisted on taking everyone to dinner at L'Aiglon. Mike gave a toast to Claire, the first college graduate in their family. And at night, as they were getting ready for bed, her face still flushed with excitement, Claire announced, "Next semester I'm starting on my Master's."

The day after graduation exercises Kramer was walking home from the college along Main Street; glancing down the block, he spotted Lance coming out of the town's only pawn shop, its three traditional gold-colored balls suspended over the door, glistening in the sunlight. Lance saw him and turned away, walking quickly ahead. Kramer called out, "Lance!" and his son stopped at the corner, waiting for his father to catch up.

More out of puzzlement than any wish to confront, Kramer asked, "What are you doing in the pawn shop?"

"I found something. It looked like gold. I wanted to see if it was worth anything--if they'd buy it."

"What did you find?"

Lance stepped into the entranceway of a shoe store and stood near the display window, then reached into his pocket and withdrew a string of beads with a gold crucifix.

"They wouldn't give me anything for it."

"Where did you find it?"

"In school."

"Maybe it belongs to someone. Does the school have a lost and found?"

"I dunno."

"You ought to bring it to the school office."

At dinner, Kramer mentioned the beads and Claire asked to see them. Lance reluctantly handed the beads to his mother, who said immediately, "This is a rosary. Where did you get it?"

"I found it in school." He looked at his mother, his face expressionless; it was clear to Kramer that she didn't believe her son and was uncertain as to how to proceed.

Lance blurted, "I'll return it. I mean...I'll bring it to the office. I'll tell them I found it."

Later in the evening Kramer heard his wife enter their son's room and close the door behind her. Lance's small TV was suddenly silenced; Kramer could hear his wife and son talking, Lance's voice rising, but he couldn't make out the words. It wasn't until later, as they were getting ready for bed, that Claire told him what happened.

"At first he said he found it in school. But when we talked about it--I asked him where he found it and why he didn't turn it in to the teacher--he admitted that he had taken it from a girl. She sat next to him in class; her rosary fell to the floor and he saw her place it on her desk. When she left to go to the bathroom, he reached over and took it."

"Did you ask him why?"

"He said it looked like gold and he thought he could sell it. I explained to him what it was; he promised he'd return it to the girl tomorrow. And he said something else--he asked me if he was baptized."

"Strange. What did you say?"

"I told him the truth--that we're not a religious family and we don't follow such rituals."

"What did he say?"

"He asked if it still could be done--if it wasn't too late."

"And?"

"I didn't want to get into it--I said I didn't know. But Dan, you're a psychologist. You remember that evaluation we had done. He's on the edge--he doesn't know who he is, where he belongs. Maybe that's why he took that crucifix. Maybe going through baptism would help strengthen his identity."

She spoke softly, in measured tones, with that earnest, reasonable manner she employed when trying to convince him of something he opposed.

"You know Dan, if you yourself converted--just went through the motions it might improve..."

Angry, he interrupted. "That's nonsense. And Lance is too young to make such decisions."

Kramer thought of the Jews through the centuries who refused baptism-- who chose torture and death rather than conversion. But yet, he reminded himself, there were those who yielded.

She didn't bring the subject up again. But her suggestions so contrary to their original marital agreements, coming now, after so many years, made him feel that a gradual encroachment was taking place, an insidious tightening of a psychological noose... around what? His own identity? His soul? Whatever it was, he reassured himself that he could always resist, that the pressure would not be effective unless he permitted it to be.

Chapter 35

"You ought to leave your husband and marry me."

Each time he said it Claire dismissed the statement with a short laugh, as though acknowledging a jest. But when alone, at times it occurred to her that leaving Dan might solve a number of problems. There would be an end to her secret life with its awkward deceptions, and Tony would straighten out Lance--who could be more effective with her son than a police officer?

But then she would lose the world of books, music and conversation that had become so important to her. And most of the time her feelings toward her husband were those of affection and gratitude, despite his shortcomings.

Yet affection and gratitude were not enough. She needed Larry. And meeting him once a week was just enough to sustain her eagerness to see him. They had finished dressing and were ready to leave--she first, then he, so they would not be seen together—when he told her he couldn't wait a whole week; he wanted to see her sooner.

"It's just right," she said. "If we met more often, we'd soon be bored with each other."

"Not me," he said. "I wouldn't be bored."

"Well thank you." Once again she tried to put him off with a light touch but it didn't work.

Annoyed, he said, "I don't like going on this way." He was in the bathroom, checking his tie in the mirror. Then he turned to face her "Look--I'm getting fed up with my wife. I want you."

At this her patience grew thin. "Listen, you've got to stop hassling me about getting married. You're going to ruin a good thing--I'm getting tired of it.

He stared down at her, his jaw tight. "I'm getting tired too. I guess I'm just a stud, that's all."

He raised his voice and his eyes flashed. "All you want is a good fuck, once a week. I'm a machine, a sex machine, in a cop's uniform--that's all you want me for."

She had never seen his anger and it frightened her.

"Calm down. Larry, please....Calm down. I can't take that."

"I won't calm down. It's all I think about. My wife is catching on. She knows something's wrong. I haven't touched her in weeks. I can't stand her. All I want is you."

It was getting late and she was desperate to leave. As she headed for the door he gripped her arms tightly--his fingers were large, strong, like metal clamps squeezing her.

Terror rising, she tried to struggle but couldn't move. Instead of hurting her he pressed her body against his in a crushing embrace, his lips smashing, bruising hers until she could taste blood. Her body seemed to melt as fear was gradually transmuted into arousal; they both pulled apart at the same time and began undressing frantically, as if there wasn't a moment to spare.

When she turned into the motel driveway the following week, her anticipation was tinged with uneasiness. Would the anger he displayed flare up again? Could she deal with it? She recognized that his unexpected anger had added the spice of danger to their lovemaking; if things got out of hand, she could threaten to leave him and end the affair. His neediness was now greater than hers; it was she who had the power.

But as soon as she saw him she knew something had changed. His face, usually greeting her with a smile or a knowing look of lust, now seemed grim and worried.

"What is it?"

"Nothing, I'll tell you later."

"No. Tell me now. What is it?"

He reached for her. "First let's fuck."

"No." She pushed her hands against his chest. "You've got to tell me what happened. There's something wrong. I can see it."

He looked directly at her. "I've left my wife."

"You what?"

"I left her. I told her it's over, I want out. I'm staying at my brother's."

"You left her?"

"Yeah."

"Did you tell her about me?"

"She asked if there was somebody else. I said yes."

"Did you give her my name?"

"No, of course not. Do you think I'm crazy?"

It was out, palpable in the silence between them. He reached for her again, overpowering her resistance, pulling her into his arms.

"Now you've got to marry me," he said.

She remained silent, still stunned by the news.

"Did you hear that? I said now you gotta marry me."

He lowered his head to kiss her, and with all of her strength she pushed him away.

"What's this all about?" he demanded.

"I told you. I can't marry you."

"Oh yeah? You need me and you're gonna marry me!"

He began undressing, pulling off his blue tie, his gun belt, pants, and shirt. She tried to rush by him to the door but he backed against it, blocking her way. Then standing before her, naked, his swollen erection wobbling as if waving at her, he said, "This is what you want and I'll give it to you."

She screamed, "No!"

He grabbed her arm with his left hand and pressed his right hand across her mouth. "You nut! You can't scream--unless you want the police here--they'll tell your husband about us!" Still gripping her arm, he removed his hand from her mouth when he saw that she would be silent; as she struggled and squirmed, he dragged her away from the door, fumbled to unbutton her shirt with his free hand, then pulled down her jeans. He threw her on the bed and when she tried to fight him off he laughed. She stopped fighting and lay limp as he tore off her bra and panties.

"This is rape," she said. "You realize that."

"No," he said, entering her. "You want it."

She decided it was over, she'd never see him again. When he called her at work she hung up. He came to her window at the bank several times; she told him she'd file a complaint with the police if he didn't stop. At last it seemed that he was out of her life.

Chapter 36

On his fifteenth birthday Lance began talking about getting a car of his own the following year. He had saved some money, mostly birthday gifts. His mother brought in a candle-lit cake at the end of dinner; Lance blew out all the flames with one breath. Kramer and his wife gave a short burst of applause, then handed Lance three envelopes: a birthday card from each, and a check. It was an annual ritual; for several years now,

Lance insisted that the gift he wanted was "cash, just cash" to add to his savings for a car.

He now quickly tore open the envelopes for the cards, glanced at them, then hurried to the third, exclaiming, "Boy, fifty bucks!"

Claire cut the cake, distributing slices in silence. Kramer wondered if his wife, like himself, was thinking of Dorothy, whose vacant chair at the end of the dining room table always seemed to assert a presence at family events. Dorothy would have had a special gift for Lance, one she would have searched out or created. She would have been a young woman now, in college.

"That makes a grand total of over six hundred dollars," Lance said, studying the check. "Uncle Mike said I could get a decent car for around a thousand bucks. That means I need around four hundred bucks next year. Then I'll be able to drive my own car when I'm sixteen."

"Where are you going to get all that money?" Claire asked.

Lance glanced at his father. "Maybe I'll work for it."

His son had never worked before; Kramer doubted that he would begin now. Lance had refused to earn money by doing household chores and declined opportunities to mow lawns and shovel snow for neighbors.

"If I can't work for it, I'll borrow it."

Claire asked, "Who will lend you four hundred dollars?" He glanced again at his father. "Maybe Dad will."

Kramer knew that if he said yes, the money would never be repaid; a destructive precedent would be set, with Lance expecting money to be available whenever he wanted it. But if he refused a requested loan, he'd be demonstrating a lack of faith and trust in his son, pushing them further apart.

Kramer asked, "What kind of collateral do you have?"

"What's collateral?"

"It's something of value that you have to back up a loan. For example, if you borrow money from a bank, you could offer a house or a car as collateral; if you didn't pay back the loan, the bank takes your house or car."

Lance thought for a moment, and then asked, "Would my bike--or my model collection--be good collateral?"

"If they could be sold for at least four hundred dollars."

Lance was suddenly downcast, and Kramer feared he had gone too far. He was about to offer his son an unconditional loan when Lance said, "That sounds too complicated. I don't want to lose my models. Could I earn the money with better grades, like we tried before?"

"Maybe, what did you have in mind?"

"Let's say I pass. No, let's say I pass two major subjects on my report card at the end of the year. Could that earn me the money for the car?"

Claire said, "Your son has learned about operant conditioning after all."

"That means you'll have to work much harder. Do homework, study--"

"I can do it."

Kramer sensed danger. "Now just a minute the end of the school year is a long way off. To reach you goal you should have a systematic plan--"

"Nah."

"Lance!" Claire exclaimed. "Listen to your father!"

"I don't need a plan! I told you I can do it. It's just two subjects. I'll have to do it!"

Kramer hesitated, then decided it would be best not to push his son. "It's a deal," he said. "If you pass at least two major subjects, you'll earn four hundred dollars to help pay for your car."

"Great!" Smiling, Lance shook his father's hand, then turned to his mother. "You're a witness, Mom."

There were no immediate changes in Lance's study habits or school performance. When either Kramer or his wife brought up the topic, Lance, annoyed, brushed it aside. "I still have plenty of time."

On a Sunday afternoon visit to Claire's parents in April, Kramer and his family were greeted by a new wreck in the driveway. The battered car appeared to be beyond repair.

"What a pile of junk," Lance said to his uncle.

"It looks hopeless but it has great potential," Mike said.

"The motor is in good shape and it has low mileage. After I fix it up I'll be able to sell it for around fifteen hundred dollars."

Lance asked, "Can I buy it?"

Mike gave a nervous laugh, glanced at Kramer, then asked Lance, "Do you have fifteen hundred dollars?"

"Not yet. When will the car be finished?"

"In a couple of months, maybe around the beginning of summer."

"I have about seven hundred dollars."

Mike laughed. "That's a long way from fifteen hundred bucks."

"Do you think I could find a car for seven hundred dollars?"

Mike shook his head. "Not one I would buy."

The matter was dropped, but during the drive home Lance said, "Maybe he'll lower the price. After all, he's my uncle."

Claire blurted out, "Even if the price is lowered a couple of hundred dollars, where do you expect to get the money?"

"Maybe you and Dad can help me out."

"You know better than that," Claire said. "You were given a chance to earn four hundred dollars--what are you doing about it?"

Lance said nothing more about the car or school during the drive home, but Kramer knew it would not end there. Claire

149

approached him several days later. "Lance has his heart set on that wreck. He wants us to help him get it for his birthday."

"What do you think?"

"If we give in, our word will mean nothing to him. He'll lose all respect for us. And he'll never learn people have to work for what they want."

By the end of June, Lance's report card arrived bearing no surprises; because of his failures he would have to go to summer school or repeat the semester.

The car in Mike's driveway was evolving into a thing of beauty. Then at dinner Lance announced, "Uncle Mike has a customer for the Pontiac. It's almost finished. The guy is willing to pay fifteen hundred dollars for it. Mike says I can have it for twelve hundred."

He turned to his father. "I only need five hundred bucks, Dad."

Kramer glanced at his wife and saw that she was watching him, her face grim.

"I know I flunked and I didn't earn the money--I don't deserve it, I know that's what you think. But this is special--a real good deal, and my first car. Can't you make an exception this time?"

Kramer could see the bright smile his yielding would produce-- Lance shouting out, lavish in his gratitude, promising to do better. Yet this appealing exuberance, no matter how pleasing, would quickly fade. And he, Kramer, would have to live with a bitter feeling of self-betrayal. He thought of the early days, when he and his son built sand forts against the sea, and wished that Lance were a younger child again.

He said finally, "I wish it could be a gift. I wish I could pay for your first car." He saw his son's handsome face cloud. "It hurts me to say no. But you haven't met the commitment you yourself made. Lance--you've got to face the consequences of your behavior. If you don't learn that at home--"

Lance jumped up from the table. "I'll show you! I'll get the fuckin money on my own! I'll earn it! I'll get a job--I don't need your fuckin money!" He ran out of the dining room, his dinner untouched.

Chapter 37

Kramer was determined to break through the angry silence and get closer to his son. He sat in the living room, waiting for Lance to come home. When he heard the key turning in the lock, his heart began to pound. Was he afraid of his own child? The thought upset him but didn't weaken his resolve. Lance burst into the room, saw his father at once and tried to rush by, but Kramer called out, "Lance! I've got to talk to you!"

His son halted in mid-step and turned, sullen faced, to look at his father.

"Sit down. Please."

With visible reluctance Lance sat on the sofa, avoiding eye contact.

Kramer didn't know where to begin. Then he heard himself say, "We were once so close--what's happened to us?"

Lance shifted his body, the body of a man, and stared ahead at the wall as though looking off into the distance.

"What happened, Lance? Tell me. I want to make things better."

Kramer waited, and at last his son turned to face him.

"There's nothing you can do. Not a damn thing. We're just different, that's all."

Kramer shook his head. "No. I can't accept that. It sounds too hopeless. We're not strangers. We have so much to build on. We've got to begin talking again."

Lance sat stone faced and silent.

"The only way to make things better is to talk," Kramer said. "Can we try?"

At this, his son rose to leave.

Kramer jumped to his feet. "Don't go!"

They stood face to face, Kramer noticing for the first time that he had to look up, that Lance was now taller than himself. He grasped his son by the shoulders.

"Talk to me. Please."

His son's mouth twisted with a grimace. "Keep your fuckin hands off!"

Lance pushed him away and he fell back, arms lashing out in the struggle to keep his balance. As he hit the carpeted floor he heard a thud, and then felt a dull ache throbbing in the back of his head. His glasses were gone but yet he could see a blurred figure, a giant looking down at him. Then he was alone.

Running his fingers along the carpet surface, he searched for his glasses, and suddenly he thought of David and Absalom: My son, my son! He found the glasses near a leg of the sofa; wiping his eyes, he reminded himself that even King David wept.

For several days Lance refused to talk to them. Then Claire told Kramer that their son had gotten a summer job with a landscaping firm. "Maybe someday he'll thank us," Kramer said.

Lance was up early each morning and left the house before his parents were out of bed.

At dinner, Kramer told him, "We're proud of you." Although cool and remote, their son began speaking with them again.

But after three days on the job, Lance's dedication weakened. He stayed in bed one morning, complaining that the hard labor had exhausted him. He told his parents he hated the work, disliked his boss, and didn't know how much longer he could stand it, but went in the next day. At the end of the week he came home unexpectedly while Kramer and his wife were having lunch in the kitchen.

"They let me go," he said.

He continued his friendship with Andy, despite the disapproval of his parents. Andy would head straight up the stairs to Lance's room, and the stereo would reverberate throughout the house from behind the closed door. When not in Lance's room the two boys would leave the house together; Claire and Kramer had no idea where they were going and hesitated to ask.

Lance failed to show up for dinner one warm evening at the end of July. Kramer had tickets to a Philadelphia Orchestra concert in Fairmount Park.

"It's a long drive," Claire said. "I think we should get going. We can't stop living because of Lance."

Kramer shook his head. "We'll worry throughout the concert. It isn't worth it."

They sat waiting in the living room, fearing that Lance had run away from home. A little after nine the phone rang and Kramer jumped up to answer it. It was the police.

"We have your son here," the officer said.

"Is he all right?"

"He isn't hurt. His friend is here too--they were in an auto accident. Can you come and get him?"

Claire wanted to join Kramer, but he felt he should go to the police station alone. The officer at the desk, a ruddy faced, balding man in his fifties, radiated an ungracious combination of toughness and boredom. After identifying himself, Kramer learned that Lance and Andy had found a car with an unlocked door and keys in the ignition; they took the car on a high speed joy ride. Andy, the driver, lost control of the car and it struck a utility pole; the front end was badly damaged, but both boys were unhurt. They would have to appear for a hearing in juvenile court, but until then were being released to their families.

After a short wait, Lance appeared. He looked pale and grim, his hair and clothing disheveled. He remained silent as they stepped out of the station into the warm night. It wasn't until they were in the car that Kramer spoke to his son.

"Are you all right?"

"I guess so. It was just scary, that's all."

"The accident?"

"Yeah, and being in a police station."

Lance didn't volunteer any more information and Kramer decided not to question him further. There would be time later to find out what had happened and what steps to take to prevent a recurrence. Lance now needed support, not the stress of interrogation.

Claire too sensed Lance's vulnerability. After giving her son a hug when he entered the house, she asked, "Do you want to talk about it?"

Lance shook his head. "Not now."

"Would you like some dinner?"

He shook his head again. "I'm just going up to bed."

At the hearing both boys were put on probation. As Andy's family was on public assistance, Kramer had to pay all costs, including the enormous bill for the repair of the stolen car.

Claire was furious and insisted that Lance use his savings to assist in the payment.

Kramer said, "It'll clean him out."

"At least he should use some of his money," Claire said.

"He has to take his share of responsibility for this."

"You're right, Kramer said. "But legally, we're responsible. He's still a minor."

"Why are you taking him off the hook? Can't you see what you're doing?"

He reached out to calm his wife. Shouldn't they be pleased that Lance wasn't hurt--that the tragedy of Dorothy wasn't repeated?

"Claire--"

"Why are you so afraid of antagonizing him? Do you think he might run away? So what if he does?"

He was taken aback by the ease with which she could accept the prospect of losing their son. Yet her anger at Lance gave Kramer an odd feeling of relief. He, the outsider, was his son's defender; the alliance between mother and son, forged months earlier by the Christmas tree, was now crumbling.

"Let's not fight over money," he said. "What we really have to worry about is Andy and his influence. I'm going to insist that Lance end his friendship with Andy. Do you agree?"

"Of course," she said. "But it won't work.

Chapter 38

She had ended it, determined never to see him again, but the ending did not eliminate him from her thoughts. It was especially at times like this, when her husband provoked her, that memories of her lover returned.

With the thoughts came a restlessness. If at work, Clair moved more rapidly; there was an easy irritability about her and she might be short--curt at times--with a customer at her window. And if at home, alone, it was difficult for her to sit still--either at her desk, doing work for her course, or reading in the living room in her favorite spot, the corner of the sofa. The restlessness would propel her through the house as she looked for things to do--tidying up the kitchen, or putting away last season's clothing.

But now the house didn't require any attention–the cleaning woman had been there the day before--and she could find no distractions that would take her mind off of Him. Should she or shouldn't she call? The conflict was a familiar one, producing both the stress of indecision and the pleasure of memory. Since their last meeting--it seemed so long ago--indecision would be resolved by her doing nothing. But this time her husband's refusal to take a stand, to really confront Lance--and then his summoning up the terrible old pain, the death of Dorothy--left Claire with a quiet, simmering anger and she could not sit still.

She wondered whether she had changed much since the last time with Him. She decided to check; standing before the bathroom mirror in the quiet, empty house, she examined her hair to see if the roots, blonde and gray, had invaded the blackness. Then she looked closely at the skin under her eyes, smoothing it with the tips of her fingers; the smudged, hollow look that was always there seemed darker. Old, time was passing.

She hurried to the phone, as if in response to a sudden command, and dialed the number.

"I'd like to speak to Officer Harley."

"Hold on."

She was delighted not to be told that he was out on duty. Her heart pounded as she waited, pressing the phone against her ear, listening for clues. Then came the voice, so familiar it seemed to collapse the time.

"Hello?"

"Hi Larry," she said. "It's me."

There was only silence. She could see him standing there in his uniform; the blue shirt with the silver badge, the dark blue tie, the wide black belt sagging a bit at his side with the weight of the service revolver in the black leather holster.

She remembered the weight of the belt when she had first struggled to unbuckle it, insisting on doing so without his help, then carefully putting down the heavy belt on the plastic upholstered armchair.

Now she wondered if the silence would end by his speaking or by the click of the phone as he hung up.

Finally she heard him ask, "Are you okay?"

"Yes. I think so."

Another long silence and she realized it was up to her to say more, to explain the call after so long a time.

"Larry.... I'd like to see you."

"Is there anything wrong?"

"No, nothing wrong. I just want to see you."

In his hesitation she could hear his thinking as he grappled with uncertainty. She easily understood. Why should he once again put up with the pain? After a long pause he told her in a flat, matter-of-fact tone when he would be off duty and gave her a day and time. She was supposed to be at work on that day but knew she'd call in sick.

He asked, "The same place?"

"Yes."

Elated and a bit afraid, she put down the phone.

PART THREE
Chapter 39

Kramer first learned of Himmelshine's arrival in Nueland when he saw the white plastic letters on the bulletin board in front of the synagogue.

Meet Our New Rabbi

Rabbi Herschel Himmelshine

Kramer walked by the synagogue almost daily but had never been inside. The building, the only synagogue in the small town, was once a house like the other large white homes on the leafy street; it retained its original appearance, except for the bulletin board on the lawn and a modest, gold colored Star of David above the front door.

His immediate reaction had been a determination to avoid Himmelshine, and should they accidentally meet in the small town, it would be as strangers. How odd to now request a meeting with Himmelshine, so many years after their final, painful encounter. Kramer felt he had no alternative; only by seeing Himmelshine and returning the ornaments could he save his son.

But first it was necessary to retrieve the crown. The prospect of confronting Andy was distasteful, but a meeting could not be delayed. After a quick lunch in the faculty dining room Kramer hurried home. It was one of his early days and he had the afternoon free; with Claire at work and Lance still in school, the house would be empty.

The silence in the house was a welcome change from the morning college bustle. Instead of heading for his study at the end of the hall, Kramer stopped at Lance's bedroom and stood hesitant before the closed door. He rarely entered his son's room unless with Lance, and now felt reluctant to go inside. But he wanted to check and see if the Torah ornaments were still there.

He opened the door. The room had been cleaned and presented a superficial neatness, the bed made and no clothing visibly out of place. Posters and photographs of cars were on the walls, and car models and parts of model kits were in the bookcase, on the television set and on the night table. The desk was heaped with an assortment of textbooks, scattered papers, car magazines, pencils and pens.

Kramer opened the bureau drawer and was relieved to find the silver ornaments present, awaiting their return. He decided not to take any chances; he would hide the ornaments--lock them in his file cabinet--until it was time to bring them to Himmelshine. He carefully removed the ornaments and lay them out on Lance's bed. Then it occurred to him that there might be additional items stolen from the synagogue hidden elsewhere in the room.

After checking the remaining bureau drawers, poking through neatly organized socks, underwear, shirts--Claire's work--Kramer turned to the scraps that covered Lance's desk, wondering why his son had accumulated it all, concluding that it was mostly junk, gathered then ignored. As he examined the layers, Kramer felt increasing guilt; he was spying on his own son. He soon gave up on the desk and decided to check the closet. It was jammed full of clothing; under the pile that had fallen from the hangers was a hidden layer of shoes and sneakers and a stack of car magazines with brightly painted sports models on the covers, some strangely futuristic.

Kramer lifted some of the magazines from the top of the pile, then found a number of Playboy, Penthouse, and assorted porno magazines. The discovery amused him as he recalled the few nude photos that were available during his own adolescence--pictures in the National Geographic, and the occasional glimpse of erotica provided by a classmate or friend.

Among the magazines he found a manila envelope; on it was Andy's name and address. Kramer jotted down the address, but before returning the envelope to its place among the magazines he decided to look inside. The envelope wasn't bulky; at most it felt as though it contained a few sheets of paper. Kramer carefully withdrew the contents and found several magazine article reprints, a couple of newsletters, and some photographs.

The picture on top of the sheaf was that of Andy, standing with three other adolescent boys, all grimly at attention, right arms raised in a salute. Tattoos were visible on the exposed arms, and behind the group, as a backdrop, was a large red flag. In its center, in a white circle, was a black swastika.

His body tensing, Kramer studied the photo for a moment, and then put it down. He felt warm; he was sweating under his arms, and his glasses were misting. Leafing through the remaining papers he found additional similar photographs, all including Andy. The printed material contained references to blacks, Jews and foreigners, the dangers they posed and the need to eliminate them from American society. After going through the printed material Kramer went back to the photographs, examining them more closely; he could not find Lance in any of them.

Relieved at this, he replaced the manila envelope and closed the closet door. After wiping his glasses and finding a large bag for the ornaments, he left his son's room.

"Wait a minute."

Kramer stopped at the office door.

"This isn't over," Himmelshine said. "I'll have to contact the police."

"That's really not necessary." Kramer tried to remain calm and hide his dismay.

"My son was pressured by the older boy, he confessed readily to us, and everything has been returned."

Himmelshine shook his head. "I'm sorry––I'll have to do it. If this is overlooked, it may be repeated––perhaps worse next time."

"But he promised it would never happen again. Why destroy a boy's life?"

Silent, Himmelshine returned to the chair behind his desk. Kramer stood before him.

"I'm really pleading with you," he said. "As an old friend."

Himmelshine looked up at Kramer with narrowed eyes. Kramer waited for a moment, hoping for a dawning of recognition; when it didn't occur, he broke the silence.

"Dan Kramer. We went to rabbinical college together."

Himmelshine's jaw dropped. He rose slowly, and then extended a pudgy hand.

"Danny Kramer! My God, I can't believe it!" He pointed to two chairs away from the desk. "Let's sit down."

They looked at each other for a silent moment, registering the impact of change.

"What a surprise--after all these years! So you are a professor. What do you teach?"

"Psychology."

"That's what all you guys do." Himmelshine displayed his familiar smile. "When you quit the ministry, you go into philosophy or psychology, still searching for the human soul."

Kramer laughed, conscious that the tension had begun to melt.

He asked, "And you?"

Himmelshine shrugged. "In the same business, more or less. I'm an exile from Manhattan. A sad story. I came here from a... shall we say, a rustic congregation in Alabama, where I stayed for two years. Do you want to hear the details?"

Kramer couldn't object and Himmelshine went on.

"I had a wonderful congregation in Manhattan. Small, but intelligent. Well off. They liked me. A civilized place in a civilized city." He paused. "It's a long, complicated--and I must say, at times shameful--story."

"Shameful?"

"Rise and fall. From Manhattan to little one-shul towns. From marriage to divorce." He gestured with his short arms. "From prestige to scandal. You see before you a man in decline, but ever hopeful."

It was the Himmelshine of old, the familiar self-mocking sham eloquence. Was the aim to amuse, or were the words to be taken seriously? And what of Annamarie? Had he married her?

"It started with a woman. Isn't that always the case? One woman of many. A synagogue clerk. Unfortunately, our cantor, who long resented what he felt was his secondary position in life and blamed me for it--he walked into my study unexpectedly one evening when the clerk and I were on the sofa. I hadn't locked the door and he didn't knock. Soon the leading members of the congregation knew about the relationship, then the synagogue board, then my wife. Let's face it, blame it on the Cossack in my genes, my only loyalty has been to infidelity. I lost my job and my wife on the same day."

They were interrupted by a telephone call--a congregant reporting a death. Expressions of sympathy by Himmelshine were followed by a discussion of funeral arrangements. Kramer wondered if they would ever get to his son and Annamarie, but when the call ended Himmelshine had more to say.

"I thought of quitting the rabbinate and doing something else, but with my age and lack of training, what else could there be? I had no choice but to go on. As it is, my position here is part-time. I also sell burial plots."

He smiled at Kramer's stunned reaction. "You seem surprised. I have to make a living. I can say I represent both heaven and earth."

Kramer glanced at his watch and Himmelshine looked at him and said, "I'm sorry. You're concerned about your boy and I'm talking about myself. Let me reassure you--I won't contact the police. But you must tell your son that if this occurs again--any vandalism or anti-Semitic act for that matter--I'll call the police at once. And of course that goes for your son's friend as well."

Greatly relieved, Kramer said he understood. "My wife and I are very grateful."

"Now tell me about you," Himmelshine said.

"Well--after graduate school, my first teaching appointment was here. I met my wife--she was a local girl. Her family has its roots here--she wanted to stay. It's a quiet, peaceful life--I've grown to like it. No real problems except for my son." He felt a surge of pain, but decided to be open. "We don't get along very well. He's unhappy with the fact that he has a Jewish father."

Himmelshine nodded. "Who doesn't have problems with children? You are not alone. My boy wanted to convert to Christianity. He joined a group."

Kramer asked, "Jews for Jesus?"

"No. Kikes for Christ."

Kramer's laughter burst out, uncontrolled, a release of residual tension, and with it the realization that what lingering resentment he had toward Himmelshine had faded. Himmelshine smiled with satisfaction at the response to his joke, but then with a wave of his hand signaled an end to levity.

"It's not a laughing matter. I shouldn't make light of it. It's my fault it happened--my cynicism, making jokes of everything. My son was looking for seriousness and that's where he found it. But I can't help myself--let's face it, I'm an actor, a Jewish ham. The rabbinate-- the ministry in general--is like show biz, only more secure. You have a captive audience, the script doesn't change, and the run never ends."

"What happened to your son?"

"He returned to Judaism. Why? He wanted to model his life after Jesus. I asked him, if Jesus were to return today, in which church would he pray? My boy was stumped; he couldn't answer. I asked, 'Would he go to the Vatican? To the Church of the Holy Sepulcher? To the Cathedral of St. John the Divine? To the Al Aksa mosque? Where would he go to pray?'

"My son thought for a while then said, 'His first stop would be the Western Wall in Jerusalem. He would put on a tallis and tefillin. He'd keep kosher. He'd study Torah.' So now my son is studying at a yeshiva in Jerusalem. He lives there with his mother."

Himmelshine paused; it was getting late.

"One last question," Kramer said. "What happened to Annamarie?"

Himmelshine appeared puzzled. "Annamarie? Who is Annamarie?"

Had he forgotten? The girl who shattered their friendship?

"The German girl. The convert. Her father was sentenced at Nuremberg."

"Oh––of course. She quit."

"Quit?"

"Yes. About a month after you left, she decided not to go on with her conversion. She eventually went back to Germany."

Kramer leaned back in his chair, shaking his head in disbelief.

Himmelshine smiled. "Did you think guilt lasts forever?"

Chapter 40

They planned to celebrate their renewed friendship by having lunch together later in the week. Hurrying home, Kramer was impatient to tell Lance the good news about the returned ornaments. It was after five o'clock; as he unlocked the front door, he expected to be greeted by the rhythmic beat of loud music coming from Lance's room. But the house was silent.

Seized by thought that his son might have run away, Kramer rushed up the stairs and knocked on Lance's door. When there was no answer, he knocked again; he was about to turn the knob when he heard a mumble, "Who is it?"

"Me. Dad."

"What do you want?"

"I'd like to talk to you."

After a stretch of silence there was a resigned "Okay. Come in."

The shades were drawn and the room was dark. Lance lay on his bed, flat on his back, staring up at the ceiling.

"Are you all right?" Kramer asked.

"I'm okay. What do you want?"

"I've got some good news. I returned all the ornaments. The rabbi agreed not to take any further steps."

"They didn't call the police?"

"No."

Still staring upward, Lance was silent.

"Aren't you relieved?" Kramer asked.

"I guess so." Slowly Lance rose and sat on the edge of the bed. "Sure I'm relieved."

No smile, no thanks. Turning away to hide his disappointment, Kramer moved toward the door.

"Dad--just a minute. I guess you're wondering why I'm not jumping for joy."

Kramer stood, waiting.

"It's because I still feel rotten. It's my birthday next week. I can't help thinking you and Mom promised me a car and I'm not getting it."

"Lance --"

"I know, I know. I didn't earn it. But I still feel like shit."

Kramer's immediate response was to somehow ease his son's pain; it was the same impulse he'd felt in the past, when Lance fell from his bike, or scraped a knee, or lost a fight.

"The only reason we stole the stuff was to get a car. That was the only reason. If I knew I was gonna get a car, I wouldn't have done it."

Kramer berated himself for having blundered in dealing with his son. Uncertain as to what had gone wrong; he felt that somehow he was to blame. Perhaps he had been coldly mechanical, treating Lance as a subject in a psychological experiment; reinforcement techniques, successful in journal articles, had failed in real life. Closeness, warmth, pleasing his son--were not these the avenues he should have pursued, as he did when Lance was a young child?

He should have presented the car as an unconditional gift. It was a first car, a rite of passage for any boy. Other parents would probably have given a car freely to their child; why hadn't he?

"I'll get you a car!"

The words erupted as though spoken by someone else; Kramer was stunned when he realized what he had said. Lance looked up at him, wide eyed.

"Do you mean it?"

Flustered, Kramer could not retreat.

"Yes."

"Wowee!"

Lance jumped to his feet. There at last was the smile Kramer had yearned to see.

"Dad, that's great! Thanks!"

Kramer put his arm around Lance's shoulder; his son didn't pull away. As they went downstairs to the living room together, Kramer was caught up in his son's excitement.

"Let's try to get the car on your birthday. Can Mike have it ready in a week?"

Lance hesitated for just a moment, and then turned to his father.

"I'll be honest with you, Dad. I'd rather not have that old Pontiac."

"No? I thought you had your heart set on it."

"Yeah, I did. But I changed my mind. I'd rather have a TransAm."

"A TransAm?"

"Yeah, a red TransAm." His son was smiling with pleasure.

"I saw one last week--it's a gorgeous car. The Pontiac is old, it's too big -- it's a gas guzzler--"

They heard the front door open and Claire entered the living room carrying a bag of groceries. Before she could bring the bag into the kitchen Lance was on his feet.

"Mom! Dad is getting me a car for my birthday! A TransAm!"

Claire stood motionless, the color draining from her face. For the first time Kramer noticed the lines on her brow and under her eyes. He took the bag from her and brought it into the kitchen. She was standing in the same spot when he returned to the living room.

"Dad -- tell Mom about the car."

She was staring at him, waiting. "Let me explain," Kramer said. "I returned the ornaments this afternoon. I thought it was time to clear the air, to start afresh. There's been too much pain here. I felt if we bought a car for Lance --"

"I can't believe it." She shook her head slowly. "I just can't believe it."

"Look, we've all been wounded by what's going on in this family. It's time for healing."

"Healing? A TransAm is healing? This boy could go to jail for burglary and you're giving him a TransAm?"

"He's not going to jail."

"So you got him off the hook, is that it?"

"Yes."

"And now you're going to reward him? I'm sorry, I won't stand for it."

"Claire, this is not the place or time --"

"It's the right place and time! We're not buying a car for this boy!"

Kramer took her by the arm. "Please. Let's talk about it later."

"No. I want Lance to hear this. He's not getting a car."

Kramer knew he had to speak up; Lance was looking at him, waiting. But no words came. Then suddenly Lance turned away and ran to the front door.

Kramer hurried after him calling out, "Lance! Lance!"

Lance was running down the street. Kramer stood in front of the house watching, fearful for his son, yet transfixed by the grace of the long athletic strides. When Lance was out of sight at last, Kramer returned to the living room.

"He's gone."

Claire nodded. "Sit down, Dan." Her voice was low and controlled. "I have something to say."

She waited; he pulled his attention away from the image of his son. "Go ahead."

"You're trying to buy his love with a car," she said. "It won't work. Dan, I don't want to hurt you, but I have to say this. Lance just doesn't like you."

"Doesn't like me?" Kramer sat up, startled. "What's this all about?"

"Your son doesn't like you. He's asked me to leave--a number of times. He wants us both to move out--away from you. I know I'm the mean parent and you're the kind one. But he wants to stay with me--to get away from you...."

Kramer felt faint. Claire watched him with silent concern for a few moments, and then said, "I'm really sorry I had to tell you this."

Chapter 41

Kramer's sleep was troubled by dreams about his son. The theme was the same in almost every dream--he was looking for his son but couldn't find him. At times Lance was a young child, lost in dark city streets or in a cavernous department store, and Kramer was running and searching in strange alleyways and cluttered basements. Then at times Lance was his current age, handsome, swift, racing through forests and fields. Pursuing his son, Kramer could never catch up; the distance between them grew ever greater and then his son was gone. Heart pounding, Kramer would awaken, exhausted by the chase. At times he lay in bed for the remainder of the night, listening to Claire's rhythmic breathing, unable to return to sleep.

On days that she worked, Claire left in the morning before he got out of bed; in the evenings he withdrew to his study, closed the door and tried to escape the oppressive emptiness that filled the house since Lance's flight. The emptiness brought back the atmosphere that followed Dorothy's death and Kramer felt doubly bereft.

He could speak to no one about his feelings. Not to Claire--she seemed preoccupied and remote. Kramer knew it was because her anger over how he dealt with Lance. He avoided an open discussion with her. At best, she would accuse and blame; at worst, he feared a recurrence of her depression.

When Claire felt too much time had passed waiting, she phoned her mother. Lance wasn't there. Kramer thought they should call the police but Claire refused. "If he's brought back against his will things will be worse than ever. He's got to return because he wants to. Don't worry about him--he can take care of himself."

Kramer wasn't aware of the impact of his concern until John Bordman asked to see him after a faculty meeting.

"Is everything okay?" the chairman asked.

Surprised, Kramer said, "Yes, I think so." He didn't want to talk about Lance.

"Why do you ask?"

Bordman shifted in his chair. "Several students told me that you canceled classes a couple of times because you were unprepared. That's so unlike you -- I wondered if there was something wrong."

Embarrassed, Kramer was unable to reply.

Bordman said quickly, "You know, Dan, I like to give faculty feedback whenever I get it, good or bad. I think it's important that I keep no secrets."

Kramer nodded. "I appreciate your honesty."

From then on, Kramer worked harder at his preparations, but thoughts about his son continued to dominate him. After ten days Kramer found the school attendance officer parked in front of his house, waiting for him.

"It's about Lance's absence," she said. "You haven't answered my letters or calls. Before issuing a summons, I decided to see you."

There was no anger in her voice -- just an impassive, hard tone.

Kramer apologized and invited her in. She declined. "We can talk here."

"I was holding off replying because..." He hesitated.

Could he tell her that Lance was gone, that no one knew where he was? Should he say that Lance was visiting relatives for a change of environment, to see if another family might do better with his son? But he could not lie.

"You see," he said, starting again, "we don't know where Lance is. He left home and hasn't yet returned."

"You should have told us."

"We've been hoping he'd come back, any day."

"How long has he been gone?"

"Ten days."

"Did you contact the police?"

"No."

"You should call the police." Her thin lips seemed to tighten, yet she continued with the same unemotional, non-judgmental tone. She saw this every day, Kramer realized; it was her job.

"I'll have to issues a summons," she went on. "You should contact the police--"

Kramer interrupted. "Give me another week."

Chapter 42

Arriving home after lunch at the college, Kramer found a swastika sprayed on his front door. It was still wet, the blood-red paint dripping at the edges. Standing before the door to shield it from the neighbors, Kramer thought of calling the police, and then decided against it. He hurried into the house, found a can of black paint in the basement and pried off the lid. After stirring the settled mass he brought the can and a brush upstairs and began painting the door. For a while the swastika, now a streaked brown, insisted on being visible; with another coat of paint it was finally hidden.

Kramer decided it must have been Andy who painted the swastika, and then for the first time it occurred to him that Lance might be at Andy's house. After hanging a small "Wet Paint" sign on the doorknob, he decided there was still time to drive to Andy's before Claire came home for dinner.

He needed his map to find the street again. While driving he tried to plan what he might say if he found Lance, but his thoughts were clouded by the repetitive sound of Claire's voice, "He doesn't like you....He doesn't like you."

The refrain assailed him like an obsessive melody; Kramer finally smothered it by telling himself that regardless of Lance's feelings, he had to find out if his son was safe. Once safety was established, he would be open and honest with his son.

He had never told Lance he loved him. He believed his love had been obvious, especially during the time of childhood closeness. Saying "I love you" would have been sentimental and out of character; it would be seen as protesting too much. But now the time had come to say it.

Kramer rehearsed it over and over. "I love you. I want to change our relationship."

The streets were now vaguely familiar--the deserted factories, the junkyard with the tires. Then he found the house. The beam holding up the porch ceiling was still there. He parked his car at the curb, and remembering that the doorbell didn't work he knocked

174

loudly. Andy's mother, wearing the same lavender housecoat, peered out at him, and then opened the door.

"Is Andy home?"

She nodded and stepped aside. Kramer headed up the stairs, holding on to the banister. The music coming from Andy's room seemed louder this time. Kramer knocked on the door and there was no reply. He knocked again, louder and longer; the music was turned down and after sounds of hurried activity Andy's voice called out, "Come in."

Kramer opened the door and restrained himself from rushing forward to his son; Lance, disheveled, was seated on the bed beside Essie, who pulled her bathrobe tight.

"Well well! Look who's here!" Andy called from his chair.

Kramer said, "Hello Andy. Essie. Hello Lance."

Lance didn't reply. Essie lit a cigarette, took a deep drag and exhaled a long, theatrical plume of smoke.

Tensing, Kramer thought of the phrase he had been practicing in the car. Still standing in the doorway as though the room were forbidden territory, he said to Lance, "I'm glad I found you--and that you're okay."

The girl was staring at Kramer, seeming to observe him without listening to his words. He waited for some response from his son. There was none.

"Lance," Kramer said, his eyes misting. "We love you. We want you to come home."

Essie reached out and tried to take Lance's hand; he pushed her away.

"We know how you feel about school," Kramer said. "If you want to quit, we can work it out."

Lance shook his head. "I'm not coming home."

There was a finality to his voice that was chilling.

"You don't really mean that...."

"I said I'm not coming home."

"Why?"

"I like it here with Andy and his family."

It was a reply Kramer couldn't accept. "Why? Why don't you like being at home?"

Lance shrugged and said nothing.

"I want you to tell me, Lance. Aren't we good parents? Tell me."

"Okay. You asked for it. I don't want to live with you."

Kramer felt weak and wished he could sit down. He was no longer aware of Andy and Essie. There was only his son and his son's words dominating his consciousness.

Slowly, articulating every word, Lance said, "I just don't want to be a Jew."

Kramer grasped the door jamb for support. They were all looking at him; Andy was nodding with a faint smile. Taking a deep breath, Kramer tried to regain his composure. When at last he could speak, he heard his voice shift to a strained, professorial tone.

"You have a right to your feelings, even if I don't agree with them." He stepped into the room to reach out to his son.

"But I still love you."

Lance pulled back. "Shit. You better go."

Kramer tried to steady himself.

"You heard him," Andy said.

Chapter 43

Since the time of Dorothy's death, the door to her room had remained closed. Glancing up the stairs after entering the house, Kramer noticed at once that the door was open. He stopped in his tracks and listened, waiting for some clue, but there was only silence.

He tiptoed upstairs and looked into the room. The shades were drawn, and the shadowy darkness and musty smell made Kramer think of an opened tomb. Sweet and painful relics of the past remained unchanged: two framed mauve ballerina prints on the wall, the books on the bureau--Dr. Doolittle, Nancy Drew mysteries--and the china ballerina lamp with the yellow shade.

Claire was sitting on Dorothy's bed, staring ahead, seemingly unaware of his presence.

"Claire ..."

When she failed to reply, he reached down and grasped her arm.

"Are you all right?"

He sat beside her and waited in the silence and growing darkness. At last she spoke, not to him, but to the room.

"I miss her. I miss Lance. Both of my children are gone. Bedrooms, that's all I have. Two empty bedrooms."

She didn't go to work the next day and he stayed home with her. "Was I too hard on Lance?" she asked. "Did I drive him away?"

Kramer tried to comfort her. Lance was safe; they knew where he was. Kramer took her hand; it was passive, the fingers lifeless, and after a while he let go.

Kramer said, "He'll be back."

Chapter 44

Kramer was walking home after a meeting of the faculty senate. He had not taken his car; the May night was warm and balmy and he thought a walk might make him feel better. He looked forward to the end of the semester and the respite from teaching. Since the day he found Lance at Andy's house, he'd been in the grip of a torpor that impaired his thinking and lectures. Walking along the empty street, it occurred to him now that he could recall nothing from the two hour senate meeting, with its announcements, committee reports and debated motions.

As he drew closer to the synagogue, he wondered if Himmelshine would be in his office at such a late hour. Turning the corner to Latimer Street, he was surprised to see a turmoil of activity in front of the synagogue building a few blocks ahead. Drawing closer, Kramer saw the flashing red and blue lights of two police cars blocking traffic to the street, the radio of one of the cars broadcasting a loud cackle of voices that shattered the stillness of the night. He then heard the siren of the town's only fire engine as it approached him and then roared by, two volunteer firefighters hanging on to the rear, black coats flapping behind them.

Kramer hurried his step as barriers were set in place to hold back the increasing number of onlookers. Soon the lawn in front of the synagogue was strewn with snaking fire hoses and floodlights illuminated the scene. Firemen wearing helmets and yellow-striped black coats sent jets of water into the building; smoke rose from the roof. Flames spilled out of a shattered window and a section of charred wooden siding dropped in a shower of sparks.

A panic seized Kramer; could Himmelshine be inside?

He asked an officer, "Is anyone in the building?" The policeman, his glance shifting between the synagogue and the people gathering behind the barricade, turned to him and said, "They think place is empty."

"How did it start?"

The policeman shrugged, and then looked quickly behind Kramer. Turning, Kramer saw a short, heavy man running toward them and realized it was Himmelshine. Kramer felt a wave of relief; he wanted to tell Himmelshine of his joy at seeing him alive. Then he would try to comfort him and share the sadness of his loss.

The tragedy might bring them closer; perhaps even renew the friendship of old. He called out but Himmelshine ignored him and ran up to an opening between the wooden barriers. The officer quickly stepped forward.

"Stay back," he ordered.

Himmelshine's face was flushed, his hair disheveled. "I'm the Rabbi," he said. "Let me through."

Scowling, the officer shook his head. "Only fire personnel and police are permitted. Now stay back."

"I've got to get through."

Kramer tugged at Himmelshine's arm. "Listen to him!"

Himmelshine swung around, glanced at Kramer with wide, tormented eyes, and then lunged forward. The officer grabbed Himmelshine by both shoulders and shoved him back.

"Now don't give me any trouble," he said, his voice rising.

Himmelshine turned to Kramer. "I've got to get the Torahs."

The flames, now spurting out of shattered windows, were lapping upward toward the roof, obscuring the gold-colored Star of David. Himmelshine stared at the conflagration, his face contorted with anguish. He turned to Kramer, his look silently imploring. "The Torahs ..."

Kramer reached out to restrain him. "You'll get new Torahs!"

Himmelshine gave Kramer a quick glance, and then tried to pull away, almost freeing himself from Kramer's grasp. Extending his arms, Kramer encircled Himmelshine's short, heavy body in a tight grip that grew into an embrace.

"Don't do it, Herschel. There are many Torahs; there is only one you."

For a moment Himmelshine seemed to hesitate, the tension ebbing from his body. Then with a spurt of animal strength, he yanked himself free and burrowed through the crowd to an opening. He ran toward the open synagogue door, pursued by a fireman who dashed after him into the burning building.

"That guy's a nut," the policeman muttered to Kramer.

"He's lucky if he gets out of there alive."

A crowd now gathered, with everyone's eyes riveted on the open doorway. Time was frozen; the wait seemed endless. At last a moving form appeared in the dark smoke and the fireman emerged, with Himmelshine slung over his shoulder like a heavy sack.

Chapter 45

As they rolled the gurney into the ambulance Kramer tried to push closer, but the police held him back.

He shouted, "Is he alive?"

The two men in white ignored him, moving quickly, slamming shut the ambulance door, and then speeding off with siren wailing.

Kramer turned and made his way through the crowd; he wanted to hurry home, get into his car and drive to the hospital.

The night streets beyond the fire were empty and silent, although a reddish glow was visible in the sky. As Kramer approached his house he saw that all the first floor lights were on. Claire was probably still up. He stood in the driveway, opened the car door, then realized his wife would be upset by the sound of the car being driven off in the middle of the night. He decided to enter the house, give a quick explanation, then leave.

She was in the living room, waiting for him. Instead of showing concern over the lateness of his arrival, she was smiling.

"Lance is back," she whispered, raising her fingers to her lips. "He's asleep."

Kramer followed her into the kitchen where they could speak more freely. "What happened?"

"He showed up about an hour ago. You said he'd return--you were right."

"Is he okay?"

"Bedraggled, filthy, but fine. I'm so relieved, you have no idea. He said he's home for good--he wants to turn a new leaf. I think he's changed. He insisted that I wake him up in the morning so he can go to school. Can you believe it? He says he has to get his high school diploma. He really means it."

Kramer's thoughts whirled in confusion. It was all too much to absorb --the fire, Himmelshine, and now his son, home at last.

Claire asked, "Aren't you glad he's back?"

"Of course!"

"He's definitely changed. I can see it. I think he'll be all right." She laughed softly. "He showed up at the door with a bag of filthy clothes--at first I thought he was just dropping off his laundry!"

Kramer was only half-listening to his wife. He wondered if there was some mystical connection between Lance's sudden appearance and Himmelshine's fate. Was Himmelshine dead? Had his life been taken as the price for Lance's return? The picture of the burning synagogue flashed through his mind. Perhaps Lance was indeed transformed--a divine reward for Himmelshine's attempt to save the Torah scrolls. Kramer recalled a legend: when the Temple was destroyed by the Romans, the Torah scrolls were consumed by fire, but the letters on the parchment survived, rising heavenward...

"Aren't you listening?" Claire asked.

"Yes, yes. I'm just very tired. It's been a long, difficult day."

"Lance was tired too. He went straight to bed after a shower. I put his laundry in the basement. Strange—it smelled of gasoline."

"Gasoline?"

Kramer was startled into full alertness; heart pounding, he rose from the kitchen table and hurried down the basement stairs. The green plastic trash bag filled with laundry lay on the cement floor near the washing machine; bending over it, Kramer could detect the gasoline odor. He lifted the bag and emptied the contents on the basement floor. The odor was stronger now; sifting through the crumpled, soiled clothes he found a pair of scorched jeans.

Claire was standing beside him, watching. He rose and handed the jeans to her.

"I passed a fire on my way home tonight," he said.

Claire gasped, covered her mouth with her hand, then whispered, "Do you think he did it?"

Kramer was silent.

Claire said, "Maybe it was just a coincidence." She examined the blackened edge of a frayed trouser leg. "Where was the fire?"

"On Latimer Street. The synagogue."

Kramer ran up the basement stairs and Claire hurried to reach him.

"What are you going to do?" she demanded.

"I have to talk to Lance."

"Wait." She grasped Kramer's arm. "He's asleep!"

"I'll wake him up. I have to talk to him."

"Please Dan. Let him sleep. Talk to him in the morning."

"I've got to find out."

Claire stood before him blocking his way; he moved her aside, hurried up the stairs to the second floor and opened the door to Lance's room without knocking. The hall light pierced the darkness, illuminating Lance's face; sleep had softened his son's features, making him look younger. If only he were a little boy again, Kramer thought.

He turned on the desk lamp, then whispered, "Lance ..."

Claire stood in the doorway, silently watching. Kramer called out again, louder, and his son began to stir; rubbing his eyes, he looked up at his father.

"I have to talk to you, son."

Rubbing his eyes again, Lance rose with effort, and then sat on the edge of the bed. The little boy quality that had momentarily charmed Kramer was gone; now his son was a young man, broad shouldered, the hard planes of adulthood returning to his face.

"What's going on?"

Kramer felt his heart pounding, his respiration growing more rapid. He wanted to ask the question at once but held himself back. It was important to proceed slowly and not shock his son into an immediate denial. The thought of being artful repelled Kramer, but he had to find the truth.

"It's good to see you back."

Lance turned aside with a boyish smile. "Yeah. I decided I've had it. I want to start all over. I'm going back to school. Did Mom tell you?"

"Yes."

"I wanna start tomorrow morning. I have a lot of work to make up." He reached for the bedcovers. "I ought to get back to sleep."

"That's right," Claire said.

"Of course. But first tell me -- what happened? What brought about this change?"

"I just got fed up, staying with Andy. I realized I needed my education -- my high school diploma -- if I was to get anywhere in life. That's all."

"Why tonight? What happened?"

"Nothing. Nothing happened. Shit, I just decided, that's all."

Kramer felt the pulse throbbing in his ears.

"Lance -- there was a fire on Latimer Street tonight. I passed it on my way home. What do you know about it?"

"Nothing. Nothing at all."

"Your laundry, Lance. It smells of gasoline. And your jeans -- they're scorched."

Lance was silent. Kramer waited, hoping for an explanation, some excuse, yet knowing as the silence continued that there would be none.

"Please Lance. Tell us. What really happened?"

The silence was broken by an agitated torrent. "It wasn't my fault. It was Andy's idea. He got the gas. He started the fire. He took the silver. He said we'd kill two birds with one stone -- get the silver crown back and torch the Jew synagogue. It was his fault. I'm sorry I went along with it. I'm finished with Andy and all that shit. I'm a new person. No more goofing off and going nowhere. I really want to go to school and graduate. You've got to believe me, Dad." He began to sob. "You've got to help me!"

His glasses misting, Kramer yearned to sit down on the bed, put his arm around his son's shoulders and comfort him. This was the moment, he felt it in his bones, his son was open to him, wanting him, it was a time for closeness, a moment that would never come again. But then he remembered Himmelshine on the gurney, and as he hesitated Claire stepped into the room and sat beside their son.

"Go back to sleep, dear," she said. "You have to get up early. Everything will be all right."

She kissed Lance on the cheek, paused, and then rose. Kramer stood in the doorway looking at his son, then left the room with his wife.

In their bedroom, Claire said, "I think we should help him. Take him at his word. You can see that whatever happened has changed him. We've got to give him a chance."

Kramer picked up the phone. Frightened, Claire asked, "Are you calling the police?"

"No."

He got the hospital emergency room and was told that Himmelshine was dead.

Chapter 46

Claire watched as he put down the phone.

"What happened?"

"I just can't talk about it now."

He hurried to the bathroom so she wouldn't see his tears. Standing before the sink, he recalled the early days: Himmelshine's appearance when they first met, the bright red hair, the waving short arms, how Himmelshine shocked and amused. Finally Kramer washed his face and quietly returned to the bedroom, hoping Claire would be asleep. But she was standing by the bed in her nightgown, looking at him with puzzled concern.

"It's almost three o'clock," he said. "I'm just too exhausted to talk now."

"What about Lance?"

"We'll deal with that tomorrow."

He got under the covers, rolled over and hoped she would quickly put out the light.

"I know you're tired," she said. "Just one more thing about Lance, we mustn't do anything to hurt him."

Kramer remained silent, his back to his wife. She put out the light and he listened, waiting for her to fall asleep so that he could be alone with his thoughts. Almost at once he heard the familiar sound of rhythmic breathing and was surprised at the ease with which sleep overtook her. He knew that for himself it would be a long, restless night despite his fatigue. Images of Lance and Himmelshine flashed before him.

At first, they were of good memories, the happy times, warm summer days at the beach with Lance, or walking with Himmelshine through the Village and Washington Square. But then came dreamlike scenes no longer grounded in memory: the synagogue interior, with Lance and Andy alone in the sanctuary. A stream of gasoline spilling out of a jerry can on the platform in front of the Holy Ark. Some of the gasoline splashing. Laughter.

The massive ark doors wide open. The Torahs, shorn of their ornaments and lined up in a row, silent witnesses to sacrilege. A match is lit. Fire. Lance tries to smother a flame on the edge of his trouser leg. Maybe with the red velvet cloth pulled from the lectern. Lance and Andy, transfigured by the orange glow, stand back to watch the spreading flames.

Andy says, "Let's get out of here."

They flee. Geysers of flame shoot upward, tentacles of flame reach out. Himmelshine appears. A curtain of fire.

Kramer was unable to fall asleep until the pale light of dawn appeared around the edges of the bedroom window shades. When he awoke, Claire was not beside him. It was after ten. He put on his bathrobe and slippers and walked through the silent house. Lance's door was open, the empty bedroom in disarray.

Kramer washed and dressed and phoned the college to cancel his classes. He found a note on the kitchen table in Claire's handwriting. Didn't want to wake you. Taking Lance to school then going to work. Call me.

The police officer at the desk was a slim young man with a neatly trimmed dark mustache.

"I have some information about the fire," Kramer said.

"The synagogue?"

"Yes."

They took Kramer into a small room to be interviewed by a detective, an older man, serious, firm, but kindly. His questions came easily, smoothly, an interrogation by a professional.

"I think it was my son and his friend," Kramer said.

He gave the reasons. The evidence. The gasoline odor and scorched jeans. The friendship with Andy. The theft of the Torah ornaments. The swastika. The literature in the closet. And finally, Lance's own admission.

"Do you know where your son is now?"

Kramer tried to control the unsteadiness in his voice.

"He should be in school."

"Could you point him out to us?"

"Yes."

He was accompanied by the detective and a police officer who drove the unmarked car to the school. As they entered the building and walked down the hall to the principal's office, the students they encountered gave them curious glances. Kramer and the police officer sat in the waiting area while the detective went in to speak to the principal, Mr. Halliday.

Soon the door opened and Halliday approached Kramer with an extended hand. "Hello, Professor Kramer." They had met many times before in conferences concerning Lance.

Halliday led them to the classroom; the detective stopped at the rear door.

"Could you just look in the window and tell me if you see him?"

The students were facing the teacher, who was writing on the blackboard. Kramer spotted his son at once, the muscular shoulders, and the light brown hair.

"He's in the last seat -- in the row near the windows."

The detective stepped to the door, studied the room interior for a moment, and then turned to Kramer.

"The tall boy with the blondish hair?"

Kramer swallowed and his eyes misted. "Yes."

Halliday entered the front door of the classroom while Kramer, the detective and the officer waited in the hall. The principal spoke briefly the teacher, who then turned to the class and asked Lance to come forward. As he left the classroom with the principal, Lance appeared surprised when he saw the men waiting in the hall. Then he noticed his father.

"Hi Dad," he said.

Chapter 47

There was a message from Claire on the answering machine. I've been trying to get you. Please call. Kramer slumped into the blue upholstered chair in the living room. He couldn't call his wife; the news had to be conveyed in person. He sat listening to the empty house, chilled by the memory of the stunned look on Lance's face as he was led away, a tall boy between two shorter, stocky men. Again Kramer saw the car drive off, his son staring at him through the rear side window.

He heard the key in the front door. As soon as Claire saw him she asked, "Did you get my message?"

"Yes."

She stood in the middle of the living room, looking at him. "What's the matter? Is Lance home?"

"No."

"Do you know where he is?"

"He's in the juvenile detention center."

Her body seemed to suddenly grow heavy as she sat down on the sofa.

"What happened?"

"I went to the police."

She covered her mouth with her hand, and then began to cry. He should comfort her, Kramer thought, but a dark inertia gripped him. He could only watch her in silence as he thought of his son. After a while she reached for her handkerchief and dabbed her eyes; the crying fell to a whimper.

"I was hoping we might give him another chance," she said. She looked up at Kramer, her eyes red. "You did what you had to do. It must have been hard for you."

He took off his glasses and buried his face in his hands.

Claire said, "Maybe if we had both been tougher, stronger, all this wouldn't have happened. Maybe you were too good to him -- you just couldn't help being that way." Her voice was low and remote. "Maybe you wanted his love too much and he just didn't like you. Isn't that odd, for a boy not to like his father?"

She silent for a few moments, looking pensive, then said softly, as though speaking to herself, "Maybe Mom and Dad are right -- all this trouble because I married a Jew..."

Startled, he looked up at her. "Oh," she said, as though suddenly aware of his presence. "I'm sorry...."

He was staring at her, as at someone vaguely recognized from a distant past. She hurried to his side and put her hand on his shoulder.

"I didn't mean it."

Without thought he recoiled from her touch. Then observing her closely, he studied the lined face, the frightened eyes; did he really know her?

Again she said, "I'm sorry." It was the hollow voice of a stranger.

"Please talk to me," she said.

His body felt heavy. He remained silent, and then spoke at last. "I'm very confused. I have to think about things."

With effort, he rose and went to his study, feeling her eyes on him as he climbed the stairs.

Chapter 48

He was running, trying to catch up with Himmelshine.

"Hurry," Himmelshine said. "They're coming closer."

He tried to push his body harder, to urge his legs forward, but a sluggishness held him back. He seemed to be moving in slow motion.

He glanced over his shoulder. They were now close enough for him to see Andy's knowing smile. Lance was running beside Andy, and Claire was right behind them. In the distance, against the gray sky, he saw the flames and a pillar of dark smoke rising in a column, as though from tall chimney.

"Hurry," Himmelshine said. In his arms he held a Torah clad in a blue velvet mantle, embracing it as one would a child, yet he ran without difficulty, while Kramer struggled as if wading through a sea of molasses.

Then he saw the red TransAm. He shouted to Himmelshine, "Let's drive!"

They got into the car, Kramer behind the wheel, Himmelshine squeezing in beside him, clutching the Torah. Kramer turned on the ignition and they began moving, but the car too was sluggish even though it looked brand new. Kramer pressed the accelerator to the floor and the car crawled forward as though pulling a massive weight. Kramer glanced back; the pursuers had drawn closer, Lance now in the lead.

"We're too heavy," Kramer said. "Unload the Torah."

"No," Himmelshine said.

The car began heaving from side to side. Lance, Andy and Claire were holding on to the rear bumper, rocking the car back and forth, back and forth...

Claire was leaning over him, her arm on his shoulder, shaking him. "Dan," she said. "Dan...."

Stuporous, not fully awake, he rolled over to her.

191

"Dan, you've got to talk to me. I've been up all night." He opened his eyes and was barely able to see her in the darkness.

"I can't take it anymore," she said. "This silence. Are you punishing me? For what I said? I told you I was sorry. I told you I didn't mean it. Isn't that enough? How long does this go on?"

"I'm not punishing you."

"But you're upset, that's obvious."

"Yes."

"Then why don't you talk about it? I just can't stand your silence."

"I have nothing to say."

"Nothing? Is it because you can't say it? Do you think my parents don't like Jews? That I don't? Is that it?"

"I don't know."

"Well it's not true. We have nothing against Jews. What I said was just talk -- idle, ordinary talk. Talk you hear that doesn't mean anything."

"I understand."

"I hope you do. I can't believe that you'd react this way to a casual comment. Maybe you're upset about Lance. Could that be it?"

"Of course I'm upset about Lance."

"I know you are. But you had to do it. It had to be done. We've just got to accept it and hope for the best. Don't you see? All that we have now is each other."

She slid down beside him, her hand stroking his face, his beard. He felt her fingers trailing down his chest, reaching for him, caressing, lingering. It surprised him; recently she had become physically inaccessible, remote. He told himself he should respond, but remained tight and still.

After a while she asked softly, "What are you thinking?"

He hesitated, and then told her, "I'm thinking of you. Of Lance. Of Himmelshine."

"Who is Himmelshine?"

"The rabbi who died in the fire. I knew him."

"Oh."

"We went to school together. Rabbinical college."

He felt her startle. "Rabbinical college? You were going to be a rabbi?"

"Yes."

"You never told me that."

"It was a long time ago." He waited, and when she remained silent he continued, "He was my friend. I miss him. I keep thinking about him. He didn't have to die in that fire. I was there -- I saw him go back in -- he wanted to save the Torahs. It was idiotic. I keep thinking about it, seeing it over and over."

She was sitting up in bed now, looking down at him in the darkness.

"A lot has happened," he said. "I feel very confused."

He sensed that she was waiting, intent on his every word.

After a pause he said, "I need to think things through. To get away for a while and just think."

"Can I go with you?"

He was silent.

"You don't want me to come."

He waited, and then said, "I have to do this alone." He paused. "Maybe we should separate for a while."

The dawn was coming in; he could see her more clearly now, sitting cross-legged in her short white nightgown, looking down at him. She wiped her eyes with the back of her hand.

"I don't think I could take it," she said.

He felt a stab of concern, recalling what happened after Dorothy's death.

They were both silent, and then she said, "If I try to stop you, it will only make things worse. If you really want to separate..."

"I must."

"Is that what you really want?"

"Yes."

She sat quiet and still and began to cry. Then suddenly, sobbing, she bent over him, striking with both fists.

"Mom and Dad were right! Mom and Dad were right!"

After a hesitant moment she looked up with a triumphant smile and shouted, "I don't need you! I have somebody else!"

Chapter 49

He spent the following night at a motel near campus; it was less than five minutes from home, yet he felt he was hundreds of miles away. After breakfast he got into his car and drove to Philadelphia, the nearest community with a Jewish cemetery. The day was sunny and warm; spring blanketed the Chester County countryside. Kramer drove past farms and estates with his car window wide open, letting in the fragrance of newly cut grass. Eventually he reached the built up areas of the Main Line, then Philadelphia.

To get to the funeral home on North Broad Street he had to drive through Logan; he went a few blocks out of his way so that he could see once again the streets of his childhood. The shops -- the delicatessen, butcher, bakery -- they were all still there, but with different owners and customers, mostly Asian. This was the street he took with his father on their early morning walks to the synagogue. He had not seen the synagogue for many years; now there was a large sign over the door, in both flowing Asian characters and English, identifying the building as a Korean church.

The funeral home was a modern building of gray stone and glass. Kramer was directed by a man in a black suit to one of the smaller chapels. Only a few people were present, speaking in hushed tones, seated in pews facing a wooden coffin draped by a black and white striped prayer shawl. In the front row sat two young men, both redheads -- Himmelshine's twin sons.

Kramer joined the small line of people waiting to meet the mourners, and was struck by the resemblance between the sons and their father as a young man.

When he reached the twins he extended his hand. "I'm Dan Kramer," he said. "I was a schoolmate of your father's."

They both nodded and Kramer wondered if Himmelshine had ever spoken of him.

"I was also his friend," Kramer heard himself say. "I loved your father."

The brief ceremony was conducted by a tall, black-bearded rabbi, a representative of the Philadelphia Rabbinical Society.

"I did not know Rabbi Himmelshine," he said. "He was a member of our organization, but never attended meetings. He wasn't close to any of us; he was a man of mystery, an iconoclast, someone who went his own way. Only in death did he reveal himself. He died so that Torah might survive. Like Rabbi Akiba, Rabbi Himmelshine gave his life Al Kiddush HaShem, for the Sanctification of the Holy Name. In Jewish tradition, there is no act more noble, more inspiring of awe. Now we know who Rabbi Himmelshine was; we know the loss we have sustained."

Kramer followed the hearse and a limousine to the cemetery. The cars pulled up on one side of a narrow path; Kramer walked with the others through a section of monuments, then stood near the two sons before the freshly dug grave. It had gotten quite warm and the sky was a clear blue; two birds in a tall oak near the path broke the silence.

The Rabbi chanted the traditional prayer, "God Full of Compassion," and their voices blending, the twins recited the Mourner's Kaddish.

Two workmen stepped forward and lowered the coffin into the grave, and then each twin took his turn in casting a spadeful of earth upon the coffin. As the group walked back to the waiting cars, Kramer hurried to catch up with Himmelshine's two sons.

"Can I be of any assistance?" he asked.

They both shook their heads, continuing to walk is silence, and Kramer was gripped by a sudden fear that he might lose them.

He asked, "Where are you going?"

"To Dad's house," one said. "For Shiva."

"Will someone take you? Do you need a ride?"

One twin glanced at the other. "We planned to get a cab at the funeral home."

"That's over an hour's ride. It'll cost you a fortune. Let me take you."

The twins sat together in the back seat of the car and Kramer didn't want to intrude upon their silence. When they were finally out of the heavy Philadelphia traffic and driving through the Chester County countryside, one of the sons asked Kramer, "How did you meet Dad?"

"I'll never forget it," Kramer said. "It was my first day at the rabbinical college. Your father was an older student -- he took me under his wing, introduced me, showed me the ropes."

The twins asked additional questions and Kramer grew more animated, fed by the affectionate laughter of the sons as he described the exploits of their father. Himmelshine's presence -- the look, the sound of his voice -- seemed to materialize in their midst as Kramer recounted the past.

"You are both replicas of your dad," he told them. "A bit slimmer, but you look exactly like he did when we first met."

They told Kramer their names: David and Jonathan. David was the student at the yeshiva in Jerusalem. Jonathan had joined him but then left.

"I've tried them all," Johnathan said. "Buddhism, Christianity, Judaism..."

Kramer asked, "Have you made a choice?"

"I've decided against all of them."

"Really?"

"No religion at all," Jonathan said. "I'll just be an Israeli Jew. You can have a secular Jewish identity in Israel."

"And what of God?"

"I've stopped wondering who God is. I just had to figure out who I am."

David turned to his brother and asked, "What about Shiva? Why did you say Kaddish?"

"Because it's the right thing to do. I want to pay my respects to Dad and that's the best way I know. It's like reciting a poem, or playing Taps... it has nothing to do with God."

They drove on in silence, and then Kramer asked, "Are you both remaining in Israel?"

Yes," Jonathan said. "You'll have to visit us."

"When are you leaving?"

"In ten days."

The twins directed Kramer to a brick rancher on Latimer Street, two blocks from the synagogue. He had often walked by the house, never knowing that Himmelshine lived there, alone.

Kramer pulled up in the driveway, preparing himself to say goodbye; he suddenly realized he might never see Himmelshine's sons again.

As they stepped out of the car David said, "Please come in for a while."

Eager to accept the invitation, Kramer was about join the twins when he was seized by a wave of anxiety.

The invitation was repeated. "Won't you come in?"

Kramer blurted, "I can't." He wanted to leave as quickly as possible. The twins waved to him as he backed out of the driveway into the street.

The fantasy had come to him in a flash; he saw himself entering Himmelshine's house and remaining with Himmelshine's sons forever. Lance would be gone, out of his life. The temptation and dread of it were too much to bear. Trembling, he pulled up to the curb on Latimer Street and waited for his anxiety to subside.

When he felt he could go on, he drove past the gutted synagogue, now roped off with yellow police tape. Reaching his own house, he was about to turn into the driveway when he suddenly remembered he no longer lived there. His hands still trembling, he pressed on the accelerator to get away.

Chapter 50

With exams over, the college building was dead, and as he walked down empty halls Kramer's feeling of isolation was magnified by the ghostly atmosphere. The air was heavy with the silence of absent student voices. Doors hung open, lifeless, exposing classrooms now vacant, as if abandoned by flight from an approaching enemy. Tom Bordman was still in his office, sitting behind his desk.

"Do you have a minute?" Kramer asked.

Bordman looked up from a pile of papers and nodded.

At first Kramer tried to explain his canceled classes.

"A family crisis."

"I hope things worked out," Bordman said. A sheet of paper in his hand, the chairman was eager to get back to work.

"I'd like to take a leave of absence," Kramer said.

"Oh. When?"

"This fall."

Bordman raised his eyebrows. "Your schedule is all set. I gave you the classes and hours you requested."

"I know. But I have to get away."

Frowning and slowly shaking his head, Bordman looked down at the pile of papers on his desk.

Kramer said, "I realize I'm not giving you adequate notice."

"You're not. I'm still trying to fill a sabbatical. Could you wait a year?"

"I can't."

"What's so urgent?"

Kramer hesitated, and then said, "I've left my wife."

Bordman, himself married for a second time, didn't seem impressed.

"The fire," Kramer heard himself say. "I knew the rabbi."

The chairman was now looking at him, puzzled. His eyes still on Kramer, he rested the sheet of paper on top of the pile.

"The rabbi was my friend," Kramer said.

"Really?" Bordman shook his head. "What a tragedy. I heard about it on the radio. Arson. They got the two kids who did it."

"Yes."

"They didn't give their names. Minors. The father turned one in."

"Yes. Lance. My son."

The chairman looked at Kramer as though seeing him for the first time.

"I'm sorry."

Kramer removed his glasses and reached for his handkerchief.

After a while Bordman said, "I guess we can look for an additional temporary. I'll tell the dean it has to be done."

Kramer thanked him.

With the tension easing, the chairman asked, "Will you go anywhere?"

"Yes. Israel."

"Really? For a year?"

"Yes."

"May I ask why Israel?"

Kramer paused, searching for the right words.

"To find out who I am. Where I belong."

The two men sat in silence.

Finally, as Kramer rose and headed for the door, Bordman called out, "I hope you come back."

Kramer hurried down the stairs, and then walked rapidly to his car along the quiet, sun splashed street. The May afternoon was warm and the trees and lawns luxuriant with new spring fullness as he rushed to tell Himmelshine's sons not to leave without him.

Author Biography:

Bernard Brachya Cohen obtained a PhD in clinical psychology at New York University. He is a clinical psychologist whose career includes both clinical practice and teaching. Practicing in the Philadelphia area, he has also taught at the University of Pennsylvania, Graduate School of Education, and at West Chester University. A Marginal Man is his second novel. *A Warning*, his first novel, was published by Musa Publishing in 2012. His short stories have appeared in The New Vilna Review, Inkspill Magazine, *Workers Write Journal: Tales from the Couch, Midstream, The Villager, The Reconstructionist, The Jewish Spectator, Lines and Letters,* and other publications.

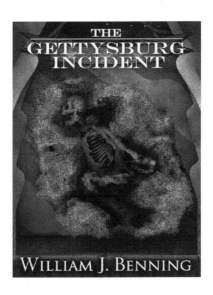

On 22 July 1863, fifty-three captured Confederate officers were brutally murdered on the orders of a southern-born Union turncoat near Gettysburg.

2013: A descendant of the officer who ordered the Gettysburg Massacre is a Senator with Presidential ambitions. The corrupt Senator is working illegally with an oil company to secure Government contracts in return for secret funding. When a mass grave is unearthed near Gettysburg, reporter Nick Armstrong stumbles upon the story of the massacre. Helped by a retired History Professor named Patrick Morgenstern, Nick begins to uncover the startling connections to the present.

With billions of dollars in jeopardy, the oil company CEO hires an assassin to silence Morgenstern in an attempt to prevent further investigations that might reveal more damaging information. The hired gun's success at killing the Professor forces Nick and Morgenstern's niece, Mary Quinlan, to go on the run.

Fleeing for their lives, Nick and Mary must solve the riddle of the massacre before the killer catches up with them.